*"The*
*You really are my baby's…*

"Father," he said, wishing she would say the word.

Ashley crossed to a set of double doors opening onto a balcony, and Hunter followed her outside into the crisp night. She stood at the railing, rubbing her arms, and Hunter found himself wanting to hold her. "Should you be out in the cold?"

When she didn't respond, he took her hand and turned her. "I'm not entirely heartless, despite popular opinion."

She lifted her eyes to meet his. The heartache and fear he saw there made him long to pull her into his arms and protect her. Which was stupid, because he would be shielding her from himself.

"This morning you mentioned wanting custody," she whispered.

He knew he had, but now he found himself unable to bear the thought of hurting her. "Yes, but I've had a chance to think and wondered if we might reach a compromise…."

Dear Reader,

Have you started your spring cleaning yet? If not, we have a great motivational plan: For each chore you complete, reward yourself with one Silhouette Romance title! And with the standout selection we have this month, you'll be finished reorganizing closets, steaming carpets and cleaning behind the refrigerator in record time!

Take a much-deserved break with the exciting new ROYALLY WED: THE MISSING HEIR title, *In Pursuit of a Princess,* by Donna Clayton. The search for the missing St. Michel heir leads an undercover princess straight into the arms of a charming prince. Then escape with Diane Pershing's SOULMATES addition, *Cassie's Cowboy.* Could the dreamy hero from her daughter's bedtime stories be for real?

Lugged out and wiped down the patio furniture? Then you deserve a double treat with Cara Colter's *What Child Is This?* and Belinda Barnes's *Daddy's Double Due Date.* In Colter's tender tearjerker, a tiny stranger reunites a couple torn apart by tragedy. And in Barnes's warm romance, a bachelor who isn't the "cootchie-coo" type discovers he's about to have twins!

You're almost there! Once you've rounded up every last dust bunny, you're really going to need some fun. In Terry Essig's *Before You Get to Baby…* and Sharon De Vita's *A Family To Be,* childhood friends discover that love was always right next door. De Vita's series, SADDLE FALLS, moves back to Special Edition next month.

Even if you skip the spring cleaning this year, we hope you don't miss our books. We promise, this is one project you'll love doing.

Happy reading!

*Mary-Theresa Hussey*

Mary-Theresa Hussey
Senior Editor

Please address questions and book requests to:
Silhouette Reader Service
U.S.: 3010 Walden Ave., P.O. Box 1325, Buffalo, NY 14269
Canadian: P.O. Box 609, Fort Erie, Ont. L2A 5X3

# Daddy's Double Due Date

## BELINDA BARNES

SILHOUETTE *Romance*®

Published by Silhouette Books

America's Publisher of Contemporary Romance

If you purchased this book without a cover you should be aware
that this book is stolen property. It was reported as "unsold and
destroyed" to the publisher, and neither the author nor the
publisher has received any payment for this "stripped book."

To my darling husband for his endless support,
patience and encouragement…and for developing
a taste for bologna sandwiches.

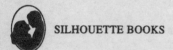 SILHOUETTE BOOKS

ISBN 0-373-19587-7

DADDY'S DOUBLE DUE DATE

Copyright © 2002 by Belinda Bass

All rights reserved. Except for use in any review, the reproduction
or utilization of this work in whole or in part in any form by any
electronic, mechanical or other means, now known or hereafter
invented, including xerography, photocopying and recording, or in
any information storage or retrieval system, is forbidden without
the written permission of the editorial office, Silhouette Books,
300 East 42nd Street, New York, NY 10017 U.S.A.

All characters in this book have no existence outside the imagination of
the author and have no relation whatsoever to anyone bearing the same
name or names. They are not even distantly inspired by any individual
known or unknown to the author, and all incidents are pure invention.

This edition published by arrangement with Harlequin Books S.A.

® and TM are trademarks of Harlequin Books S.A., used under license.
Trademarks indicated with ® are registered in the United States Patent
and Trademark Office, the Canadian Trade Marks Office and in other
countries.

Visit Silhouette at www.eHarlequin.com

**Printed in U.S.A.**

**Books by Belinda Barnes**

Silhouette Romance

*His Special Delivery* #1491
*The Littlest Wrangler* #1527
*Daddy's Double Due Date* #1587

---

## BELINDA BARNES

A romantic at heart, 1999 Romance Writers of America's Golden Heart winner, Belinda Barnes grew up in Sand Springs, Oklahoma, on the banks of the Arkansas River, where she dreamed of faraway lands, castles and princes. Though Texas is not all that far away, it is there Belinda found her prince. Together in their two-story castle, they have raised two sons, a daughter and a menagerie of pets, including dogs, cats, tropical fish, turtles, hamsters and ferrets. With sons whose interests run the gamut from bull riding to racing cars and motorcycles, Belinda is more than ready for her daughter's more sedate passions of dancing, singing and acting.

Belinda lives in Elm Mott, Texas, with her husband, her daughter and spoiled cat, Precious. In addition to fiction, she is published in magazine and book-length nonfiction. In her spare time she enjoys clogging, painting, reading, country-and-western music, dancing, fishing, scuba diving, camping and getting together with other writers.

Belinda loves to hear from readers. Write to her at P.O. Box 1165, Elm Mott, Texas 76640.

All underlined places are fictitious.

# Chapter One

"Congratulations, Mr. Morgan. You're going to be a father."

Hunter Morgan clutched the phone in one hand, the steaming cup of coffee in the other paused halfway to his mouth. "Who is this?"

"The Spangler-Moore Fertility Clinic. The in vitro was a success."

"Ma'am, this is *Hunter* Morgan. Who are you calling?"

"Did you say Hunter Morgan? The sperm donor for the in vitro?"

"No. My sperm was for an insemination on Lauren Ann Morgan, my sister-in-law," he said. "This is her residence."

"Insemination? Hold on. Let me check something. The pregnancy test is that of Laura Ashley Morgen. M-o-r-g-e-n."

Hunter breathed a sigh of relief. "My sister-in-law is Lauren Ann Morgan. M-o-r-g-a-n. She saw her doctor this morning and is not pregnant."

"Oh, I see what happened. The test results were inadvertently attached to your sister-in-law's file, probably because of the name similarity. I apologize for having bothered you."

When the dial tone buzzed in his ear, Hunter hung up. Yet the eerie feeling that had settled heavy in his gut remained.

"Who was that?" Jared asked from the doorway.

"Wrong number." Hunter joined his brother and sister-in-law in the kitchen, hoping that's all it had been—a wrong number.

Thank God he'd been in the living room near the phone. After the hell Jared and Lauren had gone through trying to conceive a child and then learning the insemination had failed, a mistake like that call could be emotionally devastating.

The phone call. Something about it made Hunter as uneasy as he'd been his first time before a judge, in his pre-attorney days. He tried to convince himself it was only a mix-up, nothing more than a clerical error. Despite his attempts to dismiss the conversation, parts of it kept coming back to him. *The in vitro was a success. Hunter Morgan...the sperm donor for the in vitro?*

Lauren hadn't had an in vitro, but the other woman, Ms. Morgen with an "e," had. And Hunter, the sperm donor, was the only common thread between the two.

Hunter knew from his own scrutiny of the clinic that an error was unlikely. Still, trouble had always had a way of finding him, even when he hadn't deliberately gone looking for it. And he knew how conceiving a child could change the course of a man's life. He couldn't afford to be involved in another scandal. Not now. Not when he'd worked so hard to gain respect and finally had a shot at becoming the next district attorney, a surefire way of proving he'd changed and was no longer a hell-raiser. He had to investigate.

Hunter poured the remaining coffee down the drain and left his cup in the sink. "I need to pass on lunch."

Lauren pulled lettuce and tomato from the refrigerator. "Do you want a sandwich to take with you?"

"No, thanks," Hunter said, noticing Lauren's slumped shoulders—the only outward sign of her anguish over once again failing to conceive. "I'm sorry. If you decide to try again—"

"We appreciate everything you've done. This whole ordeal has been very difficult." Lauren turned away, but not before he saw the tears pooling in her eyes. "I don't think we'll try again for a while. I need some time away from the stress."

"I understand."

Jared pulled his wife to his side. "Hunter, you've been a good sport about this. It's not your fault it didn't work out."

Then why did he feel responsible? Hunter thought. "I'd better be going." He headed for the front door, wanting to get outside to draw a breath of fresh air, to get away from the pain etched in their faces. And the guilt threatening to choke him.

Hunter hurried to his pickup and backed down the long drive. He had to know if a stranger had been impregnated with his sperm. Ten minutes later he hurried inside the antiseptic-smelling fertility clinic where the receptionist flashed him a smile.

"I'm Hunter Morgan. Someone called me this morning about Laura Ashley Morgen. Do you know who it was?"

"No, sir, but I'll see if I can find out." She picked up the phone and punched in a number.

A moment later, a nurse he recognized hurried toward him. "Mr. Morgan, without a consent, I can't discuss—"

"I received a call this morning indicating my sperm was used to impregnate a Laura Ashley Morgen. Is that true?"

The nurse's brows puckered behind her wire-frame glasses. "Wasn't your sperm designated solely for your sister-in-law?"

"Yes, but what about the call this morning? I want to see documentation ensuring my sperm didn't go to this other woman."

"We use a double-check system. A mix-up is virtually impossible." Opening a folder on the reception desk, the nurse scanned its contents. Her eyes grew wide, then wider still.

Hunter moved closer, his fears confirmed. He muttered a curse and ripped out the page containing his name from the file. Anger shot through him, swift and hot, followed immediately by a rush of painful memories he refused to think about now. He crushed the paper in his fist.

The nurse grabbed for the sheet. "Give me that."

"Not a chance."

"I know you're upset about this. So am I. We've worked hard to develop a foolproof system. Something like this shouldn't happen. I intend to do a thorough investigation. When I find the person responsible, they'll be fired. I'm sorry about this, but you can't take that page. It's confidential. Surely you understand—"

"Lady," he said, struggling to maintain what little control he had left, "right now this record is the least of your worries. I want to know how this happened and what you plan to do to prevent a recurrence. Give me answers or I'll shut you down."

"What about the good we do for so many couples?"

He met her gaze. "It'll be up to a judge to decide

whether this is an isolated case of negligence or common practice and if the potential for harm outweighs the good.'' Hunter turned on his heel and stormed from the building, not slowing until he reached his truck. He yanked the door open and dropped onto the leather seat, remembering another day fifteen years ago when he'd learned he was going to be a father. The painful memories of what had followed ripped through him. He slammed his fist against the steering wheel. The sound of paper crumpling drew his attention to the sheet still clutched in his hand. It felt as if all the oxygen had been sucked from the cab of his truck. He inhaled three deep breaths until the ache in his chest began to subside.

A baby. Speculating over how it had happened wouldn't change the fact that Hunter was going to be a father. Last time he'd been too young and had no say in his child's future or his own. This time, things would be different. He knew nothing about the woman who carried his child except her name, but by sunset he would know everything.

Hunter pulled the cell phone from his pocket and dialed. His secretary answered on the second ring. ''Dianne, I need information on a woman ASAP.''

She laughed. ''Is this personal or business?''

''Personal, but it's not what you think.''

''Too bad. What's her name?''

''Laura Ashley Morgen with an 'e.' She may live in Hale.''

''Do you want a partial or full report?''

''Everything you can find.''

''I'll get right on it,'' Dianne said.

''Great. I'll be there in ten minutes. Something's come up. Can you clear my calendar for the rest of today?''

''It's done. Do you want me to cancel your meeting with

that Johnson boy and the high school counselor or reschedule?''

"Go ahead and reschedule as soon as I have an opening. That kid is headed for trouble unless we can get him to find a new set of friends.''

"If anyone can reach him, you can.''

"Thanks. I wish I felt that confident.''

"Who is this Laura Ashley Morgen?''

He considered her question. Dianne had a penchant for being nosey, but this was personal. "You tell me.''

Back at his office, Hunter spent the next six hours thinking about the situation. Even though he'd had nothing to do with the clinic error, he knew everyone, including his family, would fear he had gone back to his old ways of drinking and carousing. Given his past, he really couldn't blame them. He couldn't expect them to believe those days were over. Forever.

He leaned back in his chair, rubbed his burning eyes with his thumb and forefinger, then reread the clinic's report for the twentieth time. Patient: Laura Ashley Morgen. Sperm donor: Hunter Morgan. He punched in his brother's speed dial number, needing to talk to the one person who would shoot straight without judging him. But after realizing how news of the baby would hurt Jared, Hunter hung up.

He scanned the report Dianne had given him as she'd left for the day. Since moving to Hale a year ago, Ashley Morgen had been employed at Barnett & Williams. How ironic she should work for the defense firm that opposed him on most cases. Fate obviously had a cruel sense of humor. His gaze skimmed over the information. He paused. Dread knotted his gut. His heart raced. He held his breath and glanced at it once more. *Marital status: single.*

A sick feeling replaced the knot in his stomach. He scrubbed a hand over his face and swore. Events from his past rushed at him. There hadn't been a day in the last fifteen years when he hadn't mourned the loss of his unborn baby. He'd been the only one to grieve, a fact that had irreparably stretched his already-strained relationship with his father to the breaking point. Hunter had never been able to be the perfect son his dad had wanted. By the time Hunter had become a teenager, he'd given up trying to please his dad and turned rebellious. He'd done things to annoy his dad like spinning his tires in front of Buck's law office. He'd even tried to outrun the police once. It all seemed so long ago.

Now, despite Hunter's diligence to use protection, he had fathered a child with a woman he'd never met. A single woman who would likely have to struggle to get by. A woman who, without regard for the hell she would put him through, had made him a father, when that was something he hadn't thought he would ever be ready to endure again. Especially not now when he still awoke sometimes at night with tears in his eyes over the child he had never had a chance to hold.

When Hunter had agreed to let his brother raise any child resulting from Lauren's fertilization, it was because he'd known they would take great care of the baby. But more than that, he couldn't bear to see his brother suffering the same want of a child that would never be. Even though donating his sperm would make him an uncle, godfather and part of the family, the decision had been much more difficult than he'd expected. But this situation was entirely different. He knew nothing about this woman, except for a few impersonal facts. Hunter had made a hell of a lot of mistakes in his life. He wouldn't make another. Not when an innocent child was involved. *His* unborn child.

Ms. Morgen wouldn't like his interference. By this time tomorrow, she would likely hate him. Hell, if the situation were reversed, he would pull together a brutal team of lawyers who would go for the jugular. But the clinic had set things in motion when they'd used Hunter's sperm without his knowledge. If he was more like his father, he would put his feelings on hold and view this as an inconvenience. But he wasn't like his father.

Fifteen years ago, he'd been way too young. A kid who had no say in his future much less a child's. Back then he could only watch as his and Courtney's parents had decided what was best. Hunter's father had even prepared voluntary relinquishment papers for Hunter and Courtney to sign. Now Hunter was a grown man who knew that sometimes all the medical technology in the world couldn't stop a woman from miscarrying. This time he would have a say. This time his father couldn't force him to sign relinquishment papers. He would go to any length to see that this stranger safely delivered his child. Then he would get custody because unlike his father, Hunter intended to be there for his child.

Tomorrow he would pay Laura Ashley Morgen a visit. She needed to know he wouldn't walk away from the child he had fathered.

Despite not wanting to take a child from its mother, he intended to have a say in any decision involving his child. The only way to make sure that happened was to seek full custody. He didn't want to hurt this woman, but this time he would take care of his baby.

He had lost one when Courtney had miscarried their child in her fourth month. He wouldn't lose another.

"I'm Hunter Morgan. I'm the father of your baby."

Laura Ashley Morgen stared at the man she recognized as the assistant district attorney. She couldn't think, couldn't accept what he had just said. No one but the clinic knew she was pregnant. "No," she said as a wave of dizziness made the room spin.

"Aw, hell. I knew I should have waited and talked to you at home tonight, but was anxious and afraid you'd run if you learned what had happened at the clinic." Hunter swept Ashley up into his strong arms, despite her protests, and settled her in a conference room chair. He pushed her hair back and gave her a searching look with blue eyes that seemed to see into her soul, then he frowned as if not liking what he saw there. "Talk to me, Laura. Are you okay?"

Without waiting for her answer, he scooped ice into a plastic cup and filled it with water from a beverage tray she'd earlier carried into the conference room.

Recovering from the shock of his words, Ashley realized just how close Hunter Morgan stood and what he had called her. "Ashley," she managed to say. "I go by Ashley."

He nodded, then pressed the cup to her lips. "Drink this."

Ashley sipped, not that he gave her much choice as he tipped the cup. Once the room stopped turning, she pulled away and drew a shaky breath, noticing that what she'd initially thought was anger in his eyes had been quickly replaced by concern.

His sudden lack of arrogance surprised her almost as much as the claim he'd made. She didn't know a lot about Hunter Morgan, but hadn't thought him the type to go out of his way for others. Even more surprising was her noticing something personal about the man she'd come to think of as aggressive, condescending, and disagreeable. And those were his good qualities.

He stared down at her hands clasped tightly over her abdomen, her child. Their eyes met and held when he touched the frosty container to her temple. Then he pushed her bangs back and eased the cup across her forehead, the condensation wetting her skin. His tender care was in direct opposition to the determined man she'd seen in action. "Feeling better?"

Ashley captured the hand holding the water and moved it aside. Somewhat off-balance by his nearness and her own confusing reaction, she responded with a nod. Still, she found herself unable to look away from the big man dressed in a dark suit that strained against his shoulders, the same shoulders that now blocked her view. "I—I just found out yesterday. That information is confidential. How could you possibly know?"

"The clinic made a mistake," he said, as if that should explain it all. "They called me first because your test results were attached to my sister-in-law's chart."

"That's impossible."

"I have proof that they fertilized your eggs with my sperm."

"But I talked with the clinic at length before deciding to go there. I can't believe this happened."

"They're investigating now. Believe me, by the time I'm done with them, they'll make sure it won't happen again." When Hunter offered her another drink, Ashley declined with a shake of her head. She noticed the tiny lines fanning outward from the corners of his blue eyes, eyes that made it hard to concentrate.

He placed the water on the tray, his movements sure and confident. "What happened isn't my fault or yours, but there's a baby involved. My baby. That's why I'm here."

Not liking the turn of the conversation, Ashley pushed from the chair, disregarding the hand he offered to steady her. The initial panic, which had caused the room to tilt, hadn't eased much, but she refused to let him walk in and start issuing orders the way he did on legal matters. This involved *her* child. "I don't know what this is all about or what you expect to accomplish, but you're wasting your time. You have no right to this child. It's mine. All mine. Only mine."

He gave no outward reaction to her statement, but studied her for a long moment with crystalline eyes that made her uncomfortable. "I can prove I'm the father." He ran his hand along his jaw, his whisker stubble making a rasping sound. "I don't want to make this any more difficult on you than it has to be, but Texas law gives me certain rights. I want custody."

Ashley's knees almost buckled. "No. This is my child. If it's money you want, then I can pay you for your... services."

He watched her, his gaze intent. "You think I want your money? Lady, I'm the Kern County assistant district attorney."

She returned his glare. "I know exactly who you are."

"Morgan, I thought I heard you." Ashley's boss, Richard Williams, lumbered across the conference room's plush carpet to face Hunter Morgan. "Is there a problem here?"

Ashley froze, unable to do anything but wait to see what, if anything, the assistant D.A. intended to say.

Hunter glanced at her. "Problem? No. Ashley and I were having a friendly disagreement over a common interest."

Mr. Williams warned Ashley with a cutting look before turning his attention back to Hunter. "If you have a few minutes, I'd like to discuss the Thompson case."

Without missing a beat, Hunter slipped into his prosecutor persona. "All right."

"Have a seat, and I'll get my client. I was going over with him what to expect at tomorrow's arraignment," Mr. Williams said.

When Ashley tried to follow her boss from the conference room, Hunter caught her arm, his hold firm, but gentle.

Once assured Mr. Williams wasn't waiting outside the door, Ashley glanced at the long fingers that held her, then met Hunter's frown with one of her own. "If I want to keep my job—and I do—then I need to get back to work."

"We'll continue this conversation over dinner tonight."

Ashley checked the urge to chew on her bottom lip. She met his gaze, pleased she accomplished the feat without flinching. Father indeed. What proof could he possibly have? Under other circumstances, being assistant district attorney would give him a lot of bargaining power. But not for her child. Never for her child. "I'm busy."

"Tomorrow at lunch, then?"

"I already have plans."

His jaw tightened. "Tomorrow night?"

She tugged her arm free, rubbing the spot that still burned from his touch. "I can't. If you'll excuse me."

"It doesn't end here, Ashley. I won't go away. Either agree to meet me, so we can do this nicely," he said, the underlying threat in his voice letting her know nice was the last thing he intended to be. "Or, refuse, and we can engage in a custody battle in court with the entire world watching our lives being dissected, detail by ugly detail. Which do you want? It's your call." The flames leaping into his eyes blazed blue.

Ashley knew that no matter her decision, he would play to win. But so would she. She crossed her arms over her chest. "I don't want to do either. All I've ever wanted is a baby, this baby. You, the father—if that's true—were never supposed to be in the picture."

"But I am very much in the picture. I can prove I'm the father. I won't go away until this is settled."

"I refuse to enter into a tug-of-war over *my* child."

"*My* child." He gave her another nothing-will-get-in-my-way look. "We have a lot to discuss. I'll grab take-out and be at your place tonight at seven."

She raised her chin. "But—"

"Be there."

"No, not my apartment. I'd rather meet somewhere public."

"That's why I came here today. I didn't think you'd let me in if I just showed up at your apartment. Meeting in a public place is fine with me so long as you're not concerned about being seen with me after hours?"

Ashley frowned. He had her, blast it, and from his sudden smile, he knew it. "All right. We'll meet at my apartment," she muttered between clenched teeth as her boss and his spit-shined client entered the room.

Exercising the rigid control he was known for, Hunter nodded, then moved to take a seat at the heavy mahogany table as if they had merely exchanged pleasantries. He accepted and glanced through a stack of papers, his hands steady, his thoughts seemingly focused, while Ashley fought sudden tears.

Leaving the room, she closed the door and leaned back. Her heart hammered. Her hands trembled as she pressed them against her stomach where her baby lay nestled, safe from harm. At least for now.

Yesterday after receiving confirmation of her pregnancy, she'd been the happiest woman in the world. Now that same world crumbled around her. All because a man with eyes that discerned far too much, thought his rights outweighed hers. How appropriate he was a lawyer. A prosecutor at that. What luck.

She remembered how it had felt to be lifted in his arms as if she weighed nothing, how he had held her close, made her think for a brief moment he might really care. Well, she wasn't buying it and refused to be sweet-talked or intimidated. Not again. It would take more than some testosterone-ridden attorney with shoulders as wide as the Palo Duro Canyon to distract her.

Determined to put a stop to whatever Mr. Morgan planned, Ashley pushed away from the door and hurried to her office. She needed to confirm whether Hunter Morgan had in fact fathered her child, though it didn't seem likely he would make such a claim if it wasn't true. Still, her marriage to a lawyer had taught her anyone was capable of lying. Even a man sworn to uphold justice.

Ashley had once been incredibly naive. She hadn't known any better than to believe in love, marriage and happily-ever-after. But that was then and this was now. She'd learned her lesson the hard way and had paid a high price for her gullibility. Never again would she trust a man or give one control over her life. Especially a lawyer.

And God help anyone, prosecutor or otherwise, who tried to take her child.

# Chapter Two

"What was going on between you and Hunter Morgan?"

Ashley's fingers tightened around the envelope she had sealed. She glanced up to find her boss leaning against her office door frame, his gaze watchful.

What she wouldn't give to wring the neck of the man who had caused her current predicament—the assistant district attorney in question. Of course, she would have to get a stepladder to reach that high, but the very thought of doing just that helped her remain calm. She even managed an almost genuine smile. "Mr. Morgan mistakenly thought he might have left a file here last Friday when you two met to discuss the Smither's case."

Her boss scratched his chin, his expression skeptical. "Is that all? I could have sworn you two were arguing."

"Arguing? Us? No. He mentioned that new restaurant over by the courthouse and asked if I could recommend something. Only he didn't like my idea of soup and salad bar." Ashley chastised herself for coming up with such a lame excuse. Every attorney and secretary within walking distance had already made the new café a lunchtime habit. She even went once a week. But she hadn't seen the prosecutor there and could only hope the same held true for her boss.

Mr. Williams didn't look as if he believed her, and Ashley decided she had better leave before he asked anything else. Not that she would be able to answer. The lie she'd just told stuck in her throat like a runaway peppermint lodged sideways, one more thing she blamed on Hunter Morgan.

Ashley pushed to her feet and retrieved her coat. "If you don't need anything else, I'll be going home," she said, lifting her purse and making her way past her boss.

"Aren't you forgetting something?"

She wanted nothing more than to run, but forced herself to turn back. "What's that?"

He lifted a stack of envelopes from the corner of her desk and handed them to her. "The mail."

"Oh. Thank you." Sticking the outgoing mail under her arm, Ashley hurried down the hall and around the corner. She needed to get away before her remaining composure shattered.

Steps sounded behind her as she reached the front door. "Let me remind you of our confidentiality policy. Getting involved with Hunter Morgan or anyone from another law firm would be a breach of office policy and reason for immediate dismissal."

Ashley drew a steadying breath and faced him. "You've got it all wrong. I've never seen Mr. Morgan outside this office."

"Good. Let's keep it that way." With that Williams spun and marched toward his office.

When he rounded the corner and disappeared from sight,

Ashley leaned against the door for support. As much as she hated facing Hunter Morgan, it couldn't be put off. Another unexpected visit like today's and she might lose her job.

Already two hours late for their meeting, Ashley hurried outside into the drizzling rain. Enclosed in darkness, she skirted the deepest puddles as she crossed the parking lot where a lone streetlight cast enough glow for her to unlock her compact car. Hunter Morgan had probably given up hours earlier. But this couldn't wait. If she could find his home number in the phone book, she would call him and put an end to any notions he had of being a father to *her* child.

Pulling from the lot, she couldn't help but wonder about his plans. Not that she wanted any part of them…or him for that matter. Been there. Done that. After six years of marriage during which she'd been unable to conceive, including one in vitro attempt, her husband had divorced her for the secretary he'd gotten pregnant. This same man who'd sworn to uphold justice had used his connection with the judge to make sure Ashley left town with only a small settlement, custody of her frozen ovum, and not much of her heart or pride left intact.

Since moving to Hale, she'd found a job and wanted to make a new life for herself and maybe one day a child. Now, having been added to the firm's health insurance, she had decided the time was right. Her eggs weren't getting any younger, and neither was she. The first installment of the meager divorce settlement had been enough to have her eggs fertilized with donor sperm and implanted. Unless her financial status changed drastically, this could well be her last chance.

She cupped one palm over her infant, safe and sound inside her still-flat stomach. No one—neither man nor lawyer—would take advantage of her again. She had let it happen once.

Now a child was involved. An innocent baby. Her baby.

If Hunter Morgan wanted a fight, she would give him one.

"You're two hours late," Hunter snapped, cursing himself the minute he growled the accusation.

With a startled gasp, Ashley looked up. Her hand gripped the apartment railing as if to steady herself. She frowned, then continued climbing the few remaining steps to the second floor landing.

"Good to see you, too," she said, moving toward her door. "Sorry I'm late. Mr. Williams didn't mention until after five o'clock that he needed me to stay to get something out. I tried calling your office as soon as I knew, but no one answered."

Hunter wasn't sure he believed her. She'd made it perfectly clear she didn't want to be around him. Not that he could blame her. At their meeting this afternoon he had all but threatened her, treated her as if she were no better than the accused felons he dealt with. Afterward, he had felt lower than a snake and had promised himself he would remember she was a woman—a pregnant woman. A pregnant woman carrying his child. That meant he had to get a firm hold on his temper and treat her like a lady. If their exchange thus far was any indication, he had forgotten how to do both.

Pushing off the steps where he had waited the past two hours, Hunter held out a sack containing two cold cheeseburgers and fries. "I came on kind of strong this afternoon and brought a peace offering," he said, giving her what he hoped was a sincere smile. It had been so long since he'd had a reason to grin, the movement seemed rusty, forced, and totally wrong. It probably looked as dumb as it felt.

She walked toward her apartment and revealed her surprise at his token apology only in the slight widening of her brown eyes lined with dark smudges of fatigue.

Knowing what he had to do didn't make him feel any better. Going up against a criminal represented by legal counsel was something Hunter did every day, something at which he excelled, something he loved. But taking on a slip of a woman didn't sit well with him. And something about this particular woman bothered him more than it should. It had to be her innocent vulnerability. Or maybe the way she had placed her hand over her stomach as if to protect his child...from him.

Her attempt to keep him from his child—same as his father had done fifteen years ago by forcing him to sign relinquishment papers—had frustrated him. But her gesture to safeguard their baby had also endeared her to him, making him question whether suing for custody was really best.

"Have you eaten?" he asked.

She shook her head, wariness clearly visible in the way her hand trembled as she tried to put her key in the lock. "No, I came straight from work."

"I know it's late, but I'd like to resolve this tonight."

After her two unsuccessful attempts to open the door, Hunter reached over her shoulder. Her cold fingers convulsed beneath his, but she finally surrendered her keys.

Hunter unlocked and opened the door, already worrying about how she would respond to his demands. He didn't want to upset her but couldn't stand the pain of losing another child.

The chronic self-doubts that had plagued him since meeting Ashley earlier that day made no more sense than the other things he had observed about her. Things he had no business noticing. She wasn't a criminal, and he wasn't acting in an official capacity. She was only a woman who had become a victim of circumstance. And he was only a man. Maybe that was the problem. When had he last been Hunter Morgan, the man and not the assistant district attorney? When had he last been with a woman who smelled so good, someone who made him realize how long it had been? Obviously, too damned long.

Ashley stepped inside and flipped on the light. "Come in."

In the cramped entryway a miniature flute-shaped vase filled with tiny pink flowers sat on a small half-moon table. Prim and proper. Delicate. Like the woman.

He noticed the way she arched her back as if easing the kinks from sitting long hours at a computer. "You look beat."

"I am, but I don't want to put this off."

"I won't take long, maybe thirty minutes. I'll heat the burgers and we'll talk while you eat." He refused to acknowledge the connection he'd felt with her when she'd earlier tried to guard his child. He hadn't felt anything like that…ever. He tried to push the thought from his mind. Thinking about it might convince him to go away, leave her in peace, forget he was going to be a father, something he couldn't do. He dreaded what he was about to say to her, because it would be irrefutable evidence that he truly was the ruthless bastard everyone believed.

She tried to hide a yawn behind her hand, then glanced once more at the sack. "We were so busy, I didn't get lunch either and, even cold, food of any kind sounds beyond great. Thank you, Mr. Morgan, for bringing dinner."

"Hunter," he said. "Call me Hunter."

Ashley studied his face a long moment as if trying to

read him. "All right, Hunter. Let's eat. You can have your say, then I've got something I need to tell you."

Her willingness, even eagerness to talk, came as a surprise. He would do his best to get this over with fast, because she looked as if she was about to collapse. He might be hard-nosed, but he wasn't totally without feelings. Odd that it should be this woman who reminded him of that.

Her obvious exhaustion made him wonder if maybe he should let her off the hook tonight and reschedule their meeting. But something he couldn't grasp pushed him to settle things. If he didn't know better, he would think it was fear. Fear that even though he had legal rights, she would turn this into a nasty, prolonged custody battle that would keep him from his child. Fear that she might disappear without a trace or miscarry as had happened before.

Ashley directed him to a too-small kitchen decorated with bright sunflowers while she pulled her arms from her coat and tossed it over a chair. "How much do I owe you for dinner?"

He found the microwave in a corner and popped the bag and all inside. "Don't worry about it."

Ashley dug in her purse, then stuffed a five-dollar bill into his jacket pocket. "That should cover it." She turned on her heel and opened an overhead cabinet.

When she stretched on tiptoe to reach the glasses, Hunter moved behind her. "Here, let me get those for you."

She spun around and pressed against him in all the wrong places. Damned if it didn't feel right.

He lowered his arms on either side of her, watching the rapid rise and fall of her chest as he settled the glasses on the counter behind her. Her scent, a unique blend of sensuality and wholesomeness, swirled around him. She smelled damned good.

She cocked her head to the side and looked at him with luminous eyes which mirrored her perception and wariness.

Realizing she had said something, he asked, "What?"

"The microwave," she said, her voice unsteady, little more than a whisper. When he continued to stare at her, she pointed behind him. "It dinged."

"Yes, I heard it." He hadn't, but wasn't about to tell her. In fact, he had been so engrossed in her mouth Hunter doubted he would have heard the civil defense sirens. With one last glance at her enticing lips, he forced himself to step away.

"I hope water is okay," Ashley said. Without waiting for his answer, she opened the refrigerator and leaned forward to fill two glasses from a plastic jug.

"Water's fine." He tried to ignore the way her skirt hugged her slender hips and backside, but failed. Miserably. Yes, he needed water. Lots of water to put out the still-smoldering flames of desire she had ignited earlier when he'd held her in his arms. Again he wondered what it was that attracted him to this particular woman? What aroused him, had him acting like an awkward teenager on his first date? Hell, she wasn't even his type. At six feet two inches, he preferred tall, leggy blondes who reached his shoulders. Ashley didn't come close. And her hair was auburn, not blond. Not that it mattered.

Her shoulder-length hair and wraithlike stature had nothing to do with why he had waited two hours on the steps, sheltered from the pouring rain. He had come for one reason—to claim his child. It was time he put his libido under lock and key and got down to business. Too much was at stake to be distracted by a pretty face. Yeah, Ashley Morgen was pretty, more than pretty. He'd spent a lot of time with beautiful women, but he had no idea what to do with one pregnant with his baby.

Calling on every ounce of discipline, he withdrew the sack from the microwave and followed Ashley to a flowered couch in a cracker-box living room that fit her perfectly. It made him feel clumsy and out of place.

When she arched her back again, he asked, "Rough day?"

"You could say that," she muttered, putting their drinks on the coffee table. "My boss suspects something is going on between you and me. When I tried to leave, he reminded me having anything to do with you is a breach of confidentiality. He's right, you know."

"It's only a breach if we talk about cases. Since that's not why I came, there's no problem. If you're concerned about appearances, we could go somewhere else."

"No. I can't afford for us to be seen together at night."

He fought the urge to smile, knowing it would probably earn him another of her frowns. "Because people would assume we were seeing each other."

"Exactly," she said, eyes flashing. "And I'd be fired."

"Not unless Williams can prove you divulged client secrets."

"You're a defense firm's sworn enemy."

Hunter grimaced as he dug a burger from the sack and put it on the paper plate she handed him. "Enemy, huh?" If only he could see her as his enemy. Maybe then he would stop noticing things about her, things like the way her whiskey-colored eyes reflected her every thought, her every emotion. Somehow the idea of spending time with her didn't seem all that wrong to him.

She bit into a fry, closed her eyes and moaned, then licked the salt from her lips. "I didn't realize I was this hungry."

Tearing his gaze from her mouth, Hunter's thoughts scattered as he stared at the contours of one shapely leg revealed below the hem of her navy blue skirt. "You can't worry about what other people think," he said. "Once word gets out you're having my baby, everyone will assume…"

"Assume?" she asked, watching him intently.

"That we've been lovers," he said, wondering why he found the thought of them making love so intriguing.

She stopped in midchew. "That's absurd."

He did smile then. It was her panicked expression. "Is it? How do you intend to convince the entire town that we didn't— That we haven't—"

"No one is going to know who fathered my baby." She settled her plate on the coffee table and turned to face him. "I called the clinic after your visit today. They refused to identify the sperm donor. So, you can see how futile it would be to continue to claim that you're the father."

Hunter withdrew the lone page from his inside jacket pocket and handed it to her. "The clinic manager called me after discovering how the mix-up occurred. It seems the initial collection container is labeled with a computer-generated number. But afterward, when the sperm goes to the lab techs for storage, they are responsible for transferring the identifying numbers onto the individual vials. One of their lab techs transposed two numbers. Since they must sign off on every step of the entire process, they were able to identify which worker did it. I've been assured that he has been fired."

"I don't understand why they didn't tell me all this."

"Initially, I imagine they were scrambling to discover how this all happened. When the clinic manager called me to explain what they'd found, I told her I was on my way to see you and would tell you myself. She may call you anyway to cover the clinic in case you decide to bring charges."

"Are you going to sue?"

He had intended to, but now he wasn't sure about a lot of things, including why he suddenly felt suing for custody wasn't best. "I haven't decided. The clinic has implemented a new system where they will print additional labels to remain with the initial collection and be used on the storage vials."

"I'm glad they took steps to keep it from happening again." Ashley unfolded the paper and read, pausing once to glance at him. "Where did you get this?"

He heard the tremor in her voice and knew how difficult this had to be for her. Still, this was *his* child, too. "I took it from your chart yesterday. I figured you would demand proof."

She looked once more from him to the single sheet and back again, visibly shaken. "Then it's true." She swallowed hard. "You really are my baby's...my baby's..."

"Father," he said, wishing she would say the word.

Dropping the paper, Ashley rose and crossed to a set of double doors opening onto a balcony.

Hunter retrieved the sheet and tucked it inside his pocket before following her outside into the crisp March night. She stood at the railing, rubbing her arms. The rain had finally stopped. The air smelled fresh and clean as it cloaked them in a bone-chilling dampness, and Hunter found himself wanting to hold her. "Should you be outside in the cold?"

When she didn't respond, he took her hand and turned her. "I'm sure what you're imagining is horrible. I'm not entirely heartless, despite popular opinion."

She lifted her eyes to meet his. The heartache and fear he saw there made him long to pull her in his arms and protect her. Which was stupid, because he would be shielding her from himself.

"This morning you mentioned wanting custody."

He knew he had, but now found himself unable to bear the thought of hurting her. "Yes, but I've had a chance to think since then and wondered if we might reach a compromise. I want to help raise this child, Ashley. I would be willing to give you money each month to help out."

"I don't think that's a good idea," she said, stepping back, away from his touch.

"Hear me out," he said, holding up a hand.

He tried to gauge her reaction to what he had said so far. She didn't say anything more, but didn't move either, so he took that as a good sign. "Joint custody."

Ashley crossed her arms over her midsection in a defensive gesture, the same way she had done earlier. "No."

He doubted her spine could get any more rigid and hated upsetting her like this. Still, he couldn't back down. "The baby would live with you for six months and with me six."

"No." Her eyes bore into him. "I won't give up my child."

The tremor in Ashley's voice revealed her slipping control, and he hated himself for what he was doing, but he couldn't stop thinking about the child he had lost. "I'm not asking you to give up the child exactly. I want to spend time with my baby. I want a chance to be a father."

She lifted her chin in a defiant gesture. "I'll tell the baby about you when it's older."

"When would that be?"

"I don't know. Later." She watched Hunter as if trying to read him, but he schooled his features, unwilling to let her see how much she affected him.

Before she had miscarried, the mother of his first child had been coerced by their parents into deciding it would be best to give the baby up for adoption. Yet Ashley stood firm, ready to fight to protect her child. *Their child.*

"Can't you understand? This baby means more to me

than anything. I'm sorry, Hunter, but I can't do what you're asking."

"Can't or won't?" He didn't understand the sudden heaviness in his chest or his need to touch her, comfort her. When he saw her shiver, he moved closer to encourage Ashley back through the double doors. With his hand at her spine, he steered her to the sofa. What he really wanted was to pull her into his arms and hold her, and that didn't make any sense. "I didn't come here to argue or upset you. Being a single woman, I'm sure you realize having a child will be financially draining. I want to make it easier on you. I'm offering to help."

"I'm not stupid, Hunter. You and I both know you're not thinking of me. You want to buy this child, but you can't," she said, lowering herself onto the couch. "I won't let you."

"Why? Isn't that exactly what you did?"

She flinched.

Hunter cursed himself.

"It isn't the same," she said, jutting her chin out, "and you know it. These are precisely the kind of problems I had hoped to avoid by requesting an anonymous donor."

Hunter felt like a jerk, but he'd already lost one child. Now, the future of this child was at stake. Later he would find a way to make amends once Ashley had agreed to his terms. "My sperm was intended to go to Lauren, my sister-in-law, but it was used to impregnate you. That makes me your child's father."

"Did Lauren conceive?"

Under the circumstances it was probably a blessing she hadn't. "No. My brother has a low sperm count and they thought that was the problem. Now, I don't know what to think."

"I'm sorry." Ashley's gaze met his. "If she had, would

you have shared custody? What would your role have
been?"

Hunter knew where she was leading and stopped short
of smiling at her cunning. "I would have been Uncle
Hunter, but it would have been different, because I'd have
seen the baby every day. I'd have known he or she was
being well cared for and if the child needed me, I'd have
been there." And it possibly would have proven that he
was no longer selfish and self-absorbed, contrary to his father's belief.

Ashley took a drink from her water glass and returned it
to the coffee table. "I don't think I could stand by and
watch someone else raise my child."

He had thought he could, because he would have done
it out of love for his brother. Now, he realized how painful
it would have been to watch someone else raising his child,
a child he would never be able to claim. "Then you understand my position."

"I do, but this baby is everything to me. It may very
well be my last chance. I can't—I won't let you take this
child from me." She stared at him, then clenched her eyes
shut as if struggling for composure.

He knelt beside the sofa and placed his hand over her
abdomen, ignoring the way her eyes shot open and the sudden look of panic that crossed her face. "I may not have
been in your bed at the time of conception, but I am this
baby's father in every sense of the word. I could talk for
hours about my rights as a father that every court in Texas
would enforce, no matter how much you might want it to
be otherwise. But I won't. You said this could be your last
chance. It could very well be mine, too, and I want to be
there for my child."

She moved his hand to the sofa cushion. "Children are

for loving. They're for holding and kissing day in and day out. You can't make a family six months out of the year."

"People do it all the time."

"Not with my child. That sort of uprooting is confusing. I don't care who or what you are, I won't subject my baby to that. And if you really cared about him or her, you wouldn't either."

He hated to admit it, but she was right. "I do care."

"No, Hunter, I don't think you do." She stood. "And I don't think we have anything else to discuss."

He pushed himself to his feet. "We haven't resolved this."

"I have nothing else to say to you."

"Will you at least think about what I've said? I admit that a child needs a mother, but he or she will need a father, too. Let me assume that responsibility. Let me be a father to my child."

Her sudden anger caught him off-guard as she marched around him to the front door. "Is that what you see this as? A responsibility? What about love?"

"This is my child. He or she would never have reason to doubt my love."

"Will that be enough?" she asked, opening her apartment door in silent invitation for him to leave.

He walked toward her. "I don't know, but neither do you."

She stared at him, giving no clue as to her thoughts.

When she remained silent, he paused in the doorway, dug out the five dollars she'd earlier pushed into his pocket and pressed it into the center of the pink bouquet on the table. "Dinner was on me." Then he left, waiting outside until he heard her throw the dead bolt on the door. He hated leaving with things still unresolved, but doubted he would make any more headway tonight.

Okay, maybe things hadn't gone so well, but she hadn't slapped him. Actually, she had reacted far better than he'd expected. Far better than he would have had the tables been turned.

All things considered, the fact she had talked to him at all gave him hope. And there was still time. Tomorrow, after she had calmed down, he would talk with her again.

Hunter scratched his jaw as he strode to his pickup. While at his office that afternoon he had searched for case law to support his claim. He'd ignored the ringing phone and admitted she might have tried to call him. His time had been well spent as he had found five Texas Supreme Court decisions issued on appeal which left little doubt about a father's rights—his rights. Odd that after finding cases to support his claim, he hadn't used the information. Though he didn't understand it, he chalked it up to the strain of reliving past events, events he'd tried to forget, but never had.

He unlocked his truck and slid inside. With time, he believed she would come around. She was obviously an intelligent woman who would eventually see he asked for nothing more than what was mandated by the courts.

Part of his job as prosecutor was to read people's reactions to certain events and then judge their guilt or innocence. Tonight, he had handled things badly and come on way too strong. Ashley had responded to his demands with fear and anger, which had kept her from using her head and being rational. Tomorrow, he would keep the prosecutor part of him under wraps, voice his terms in a nonthreatening manner and do everything possible to keep her from throwing up her guard. Maybe then they could talk things out and come to an agreement.

He pulled away from the apartment and headed home,

thinking he now had a better grasp on the situation. He was making progress, doing the right thing. So why did the thought of taking his child from Ashley suddenly feel so wrong?

## Chapter Three

"Mind if I join you?"

Ashley looked up from her glass of milk as Hunter slid into the opposite side of the booth. She refused to turn to see how many of the restaurant patrons were members of the legal community. It was ridiculous to hope no one had noticed Hunter's arrival, or his destination. The man stood as tall as an oak tree and had dark good looks that naturally drew attention. Not hers, but others. "What do you think you're doing?"

"Eating lunch with the prettiest woman in Hale, Texas," he said, flashing her a crooked smile that sent a jolt of awareness through her.

It was just the raging hormones she'd heard all pregnant women experienced. Under normal conditions, she wouldn't notice the tantalizing scent of his cologne—a heady mix of arrogance and potent male—or find him the least bit attractive. But from the moment the assistant district attorney had stormed into the conference room and staked his claim, nothing had been normal. And in spite of knowing better, she couldn't stop the warmth that spiraled through her or the welcoming smile that worked its way to her lips. "Don't try to sweet-talk me, Hunter Morgan. I'm on to you. It won't work."

He chuckled, a low rumbling sound that plucked a chord of need deep inside her. "In that case, I won't bother telling you how that leopard print brings out the little gold flecks in your eyes. If you were a prosecution witness, I'd send you home to change into basic black, something conservative that buttons all the way to the neck and has long sleeves."

"Why?" she heard herself ask, intrigued by the slant of the conversation and the way he watched her, the way he made her feel all warm and tingly on the inside.

His blue eyes darkened. His expression turned serious. "The way you're dressed now," he said, his gaze assessing, lingering here and there in a most disconcerting manner, "is quite distracting. All the men on the jury would be so busy ogling you, they wouldn't hear a word of your testimony."

It *was* working. Darn him. In spite of who he was and what she knew he was after, his seductive charm was doing a number on her. Hormones, she reminded herself. It was only a rush of hormones. No, it was more than that. More like an earthquake, a volcanic eruption or a tornado.

"I suppose I can see where, assuming the jurors are all males of reproductive age, they might be somewhat distracted by certain clothing on a woman," she said.

"A very attractive woman." One corner of his mouth lifted. "And what age group do you consider to fall into that reproductive stage?"

Oh, dear. She cleared her throat as she considered his question. "I assume that would be college—"

"Lower."

"High school—"

"Lower."

She blinked. "I, uh, wasn't fortunate enough to have any brothers, so I'm rather ill equipped—"

"Oh, I think you're very well equipped." He flashed her a wicked smile that warned her he was up to no good. "Try junior high."

Heat rushed to her cheeks, and she fought the urge to cover her face with her hands. "Really?"

"Pretty close." His blue eyes danced with mirth. "Go on."

How had she gotten herself into this? "All right, Mr. M—"

"Hunter."

"Very well, Hunter. From junior high school to..." She thought about it a moment, then smiled. "From junior high to sixty-five."

One brow arched, and he shook his head.

"Seventy?"

Nothing.

"Eighty?"

Still nothing.

She frowned at him. "Death?"

"Exactly. So you can see how we have to pay careful attention to what a witness wears. If the woman is a looker, like you, then it's really a problem."

A looker? Her?

Thankfully, a waitress who barely looked old enough to be out of school sauntered to their table and settled a huge glass of iced tea in front of Hunter. "You want the usual?"

"Sure thing."

She nodded and moved to the next booth.

"You come here often?" Ashley asked, hoping to distract him from their earlier topic. Funny how his smile and easy banter had almost made her forget why he was hounding her. Almost.

He took a drink from the glass and shrugged. "Couple of times a week."

"Do you always sit with available women, or is it just that you're getting even with me for last night?"

"Getting even?"

"Once my boss hears we've had lunch together, he'll probably fire me. I'm sure he would never believe we talked about witnesses."

"And sex," Hunter added with a devilish grin.

"Yes, and that." Ashley cleared her throat and met his gaze. "Isn't there some other woman in Hale you could pester? Why me?"

"Because you're pregnant with my child."

Ashley looked around to see if anyone paid them any attention. "Don't say that so loud."

"Why not? It's true."

She sighed. "Hunter, why are you here? What do you want from me?"

"You know what I want. Since you weren't interested in my last offer, I thought we might negotiate, but if you would rather I go, then—"

"No." In her haste to stop him from leaving, she knocked over her glass of milk, sending its contents into his lap.

Hunter righted the glass, then slid from the booth and picked up his napkin, still wrapped around his silverware.

Mortified by what she had done, Ashley grabbed her own napkin from her lap and stood. When she tried to dab at the milk soaking his pants, he caught her wrist. "I'm not sure you really want to do that."

The waitress who had rushed to mop up the spill smiled

as she smoothed the towel over the table before walking away.

Ashley shoved the napkin in his hand and returned to her seat, unable to look him in the face. Her cheeks burned at the thought of what she had almost done, what she had almost touched. She groaned, wondering if anyone would notice if she crawled under the table.

When Hunter slipped into the booth, he sat watching her, but she refused to have anything further to do with him.

"Ashley, look at me." His fingers cupped her chin and turned her head. "Don't worry about the pants. I have plenty of time to change before court resumes."

"Have your suit cleaned and send me the bill." She couldn't remember when she'd been more embarrassed. "I believe you mentioned wanting to negotiate." She wanted to change the subject and try to forget she had just dumped milk in the assistant D.A.'s lap.

"I still think the six-month split would work, but since you aren't receptive, how would you feel about me taking summers and every other weekend? On even years, I'd get Thanksgiving, Fourth of July and Christmas holidays. And Easter, Labor Day, Memorial Day, spring break and birthdays on odd years."

That wasn't what she had hoped to hear. Her idea of a negotiation was him deciding a supervised dinner once a year would suffice. "I know you think I'm not being fair, but darn it, Hunter, my dream of having a family didn't include you."

"Then you're rejecting my offer?"

"No, I haven't rejected it…exactly. It's just going to take a little time for me to get used to the idea of having to share my child." Then again, it might take forever.

"So you'll consider it?" He lifted his tea and drank,

drawing her eyes to his tanned throat and how it worked as he swallowed.

She noticed the rising temperature and decided it must be a combination of the crowded dining area and the cooking going on in the kitchen. Wanting only to get rid of Hunter, she decided to agree. It wasn't like she couldn't later change her mind. Her prerogative. "I'll give it some thought. It might be workable." But she doubted it.

The waitress placed a huge platter containing a thick steak and fries in front of Hunter, then refilled his glass of tea and glanced at Ashley. "Do you want more milk?"

"No, thank you," Ashley said, watching the waitress as she moved to the next table.

Hunter cut into the meat and took a bite. "Aren't you eating?"

"No." She stared at the pink liquid pooling on his plate and shivered. "Hunter, I don't think that cow's dead."

"It's a little rare, but I've had worse."

"A little rare? It looks like it could crawl off your plate." It sure was making her stomach crawl. When he cut another bite, she shuddered, wondering how he would feel about her getting sick on his loafers now that she had already dumped her milk in his lap.

"You're looking a little green. Are you okay?"

She made the mistake of looking at his meal again. Bile rose in her throat. Catching the end of the table, Ashley grabbed her purse and stood. A mild cramp caught her unaware. She remained still, placing her hand over her stomach.

Hunter dropped his fork and was instantly at her side, slipping his arm around her waist. "Is something wrong?"

Ashley inhaled slowly, then shook her head. "Just a twinge. It's okay now." She withdrew from his grasp and returned to her seat. "Hunter, sit down. People are staring."

He continued to stand there, frowning at her. "Do you need to go to the hospital?"

"Hospital? Goodness no. It was just a little cramp. Pregnant women have all kinds of little aches and pains that mean nothing." At least that's what her neighbor had told her when she'd gone over there the night before. After Hunter had left, Ashley had started feeling weird, so she'd sought out Martha, who was a nurse and had three kids. Martha had assured her that unless there were other symptoms, a twinge or two was nothing to be concerned about. So far, there had been nothing, except nausea which Martha had assured her was normal.

Finally he returned to his seat. "You're sure?"

"Yeah. My stomach's just rebelling from having to watch you eat that near-raw meat. You know, that really is disgusting."

He gave her a look filled with doubt. Finally he retrieved his fork. "A growing boy can't survive on a glass of milk…and neither can a pregnant woman. Do you always skip lunch? If it's money—"

"It has nothing to do with money. I usually eat, but didn't feel like it today." She pulled two dollars from her purse and dropped them on the table as she slid from the booth, catching her jacket. "This has been a real experience, Hunter, but some of us have to work for a living."

"I'll get it." He lifted the money and shoved it back in her purse. "Listen, Ashley, if you don't get to feeling better, I'd like you to see a doctor. I also want your promise to call me if you have any problems, any at all."

"Don't be ridiculous. There's nothing wrong with me, except a queasy stomach."

He lowered his fork to the edge of his plate. "If you

won't give me your word to call if you need me, then I suppose I can check on you every few hours."

She knew he would, too. Blast him. "Oh, all right."

His lips lifted in a smile that stole her breath. "Good girl."

Ashley glanced at her watch and groaned. "I've got to go. I'm already late."

"Here." He tugged his wallet from his back pocket and pulled out a business card, then scribbled two numbers on the reverse side. "This is my office number. The ones I added on the back are my home and cell numbers."

"Thanks. I'm really sorry about your suit." Ashley accepted the card and stuck it in her pocket as she hurried from the restaurant, intending to trash it the first chance she got. He was being overcautious. She never should have had lunch with him, not that he'd given her much choice. Still, she shouldn't have had such a good time. Drat him. It was all his fault. No way would she ever call him, no matter the reason.

She hurried down the sidewalk, uncomfortable with the thought that Hunter worried about her welfare. It also pleased her, and darned if she knew why. He was everything she disliked in a man. She supposed nagging someone to death came naturally since he was a prosecutor, but he was driving her nuts. And darn it all, she was starting to enjoy it.

Had he really expected her to jump at his new offer? If so, he was a poor judge of character. Or maybe she was different than the females he knew. She found herself wondering about the kind of women he dated and whether he had a special someone in his life. Maybe his significant other would be jealous and put a stop to any notion he had of claiming this baby. If Ashley were Hunter's woman, she wouldn't like the idea of him fathering a child with another.

Not that they—she and Hunter—had created this baby in the traditional way. Funny that she had no trouble at all envisioning him tangled in black satin sheets…naked.

She hurried inside the office, intending to throw his business card away at her first opportunity. She dug it from her pocket, then paused.

She tightened her hand around the paper, crumpling it, but couldn't bring herself to drop it in the trash. More than once she'd discovered her boss going through her wastebasket in search of a discarded document draft. It wouldn't do for him to stumble across Hunter Morgan's business card with his home and cell numbers scrawled on the back. No telling what Mr. Williams would think. She shoved the card in her purse, promising to get rid of it when she got home.

Her inability to discard the numbers had nothing to do with Hunter telling her she was a looker. Nothing at all.

At four o'clock that afternoon, Hunter had given up on getting any work done. The arraignment had gone without a hitch and he'd gone to the high school to meet with the counselor and troubled teen Greg Johnson. Things had gone from bad to worse when Greg had walked out before giving them a chance to really talk. Several times Hunter had felt the urge to call Ashley after he'd returned to the office, had even picked up the phone a time or two, only to hang up at the last minute.

Now he sat in his pickup outside her apartment, waiting for her to get home so he could make sure she was all right. He'd thought to swing by her office, but decided she would have a fit and what little progress he'd made with her would be lost. He knew his being there was stupid, but since lunch, he'd had a niggling feeling something wasn't right, that Ashley needed him. He'd always been one to play his hunches and would do so now.

Seeing movement in her apartment window, he shoved open the truck door and slid out. He glanced at his watch and swore as he took the stairs two at a time. He called himself a fool every step of the way, but knew Williams didn't let his people off this early. Ashley might slam the door in his face, but at least he would know she was okay.

Hunter grabbed the handrail and leapt to the second floor landing. His sudden appearance at her doorstep had everything to do with what had happened fifteen years ago. It also had to do with Ashley and his inexplicable need to protect her. It made no sense at all.

He paused at her door, his chest heaving from the breakneck climb, his breath swirling in the cold March wind as he knocked.

After what seemed forever, the door opened a crack.

Ashley wore jeans and a turtleneck sweater, certainly not office attire. She had pulled her auburn hair back in a lopsided ponytail. He liked the way it softened her. But the lack of color in her face made his blood run cold. "What's wrong?"

"Hunter."

He stepped inside. "What's going on?"

She stared at him, tears filling her brown eyes, her bottom lip quivering. "I'm spotting."

He frowned. "Spotting?"

"Bleeding," she explained, a blush coloring her cheeks.

Hunter's heart slammed against his ribs as he remembered a similar event from his past. "Have you called a doctor?"

"Yes. I talked with Dr. Rollins, my obstetrician. He's finishing afternoon rounds and said he'd meet me at his office."

"When?"

"In fifteen minutes."

"Why didn't you call me?"

She opened her fist to reveal his crumpled business card.

"Where's your coat?" he asked, turning to scan the living room. He crossed the room and grabbed her jacket from beneath a half-packed suitcase open on the couch. Helping her into her coat, he wondered if the bag meant she'd planned to skip town. But he couldn't think about that now.

He lifted her with an arm behind her back and knees and held her. He had prepared legal briefs that weighed more than her.

She slid her arms around his neck. "What are you doing?"

"Getting you to the doctor." He locked her door and navigated the stairs, careful not to jostle her.

"Hunter?" she said, her breath warm on his cheek.

"Yes."

"I'm scared," she said, settling her head against his shoulder. "Really, really scared."

Hunter's gut clenched as he rounded the passenger side of his truck. Opening the door, he lay her across the bench seat, noticing again how fragile she looked. "Me, too, Ashley. Me, too."

The extent of his fear for her frightened him more than any murderer or hardened criminal he had ever faced. In court he was on his turf and could handle anything that came his way. But now when it really mattered—when his child's life hung in the balance—he felt inadequate, helpless. He had thought he would make things right by maintaining control. Only now did he realize he had no influence over fate.

Hunter couldn't change his past or make up to his family for all the hell he had put them through in his rebellious days. And he couldn't bring back the child he had lost, but he damned well would do right by this baby. And Ashley.

For now all he could do was get her to the hospital and stay by her side until they knew something. And if by some miracle the doctor could stop the bleeding, then he would take care of her, no matter how much she argued. At least until his baby's birth. And after that, too, if she would let him. Because, no matter what might develop between him and Ashley in the future, she was now and would always be the mother of his child.

Ashley pushed herself higher on the examining table. The doctor visits, daily injections of first one drug and then another, the tedious waiting for test results, always ending in bad news had taken its toll. Now, having gotten pregnant, she wasn't sure she wanted to hear what Dr. Rollins had to say. She pulled the sheet higher even though her trembling had nothing to do with the cold air blowing from the overhead vent.

The obstetrician pulled off his rubber gloves and dropped them in the trash receptacle. "I'm not finding anything that causes me concern; however, I would like to do an ultrasound to see if it shows anything out of the ordinary. Why don't we bring the father in for that before he wears a path in my carpet."

Ashley bit her tongue to keep from saying no. Hunter was the father, a father who, as he'd pointed out, had certain rights, rights she'd tried to ignore. The idea of him in the room with her wearing only a paper hospital gown beneath a too-small sheet didn't do anything to soothe her already frayed nerves. She believed it best if he stayed in the other room, but found herself nodding agreement for him to join them.

On more than one occasion, he had knocked her legs

from beneath her with his unreasonable demands. But then today he'd comforted her, remained at her side until she'd insisted he leave. He was certainly a study in contradiction. In spite of their disagreement over his involvement in her child's life, he had allowed her brief glimpses of a tender, caring side buried beneath the prosecutor facade. Though they had yet to reach any agreement, she needed him nearby to help her through this ordeal.

After scribbling a note on her chart, Dr. Rollins and his nurse stepped from the room, leaving Ashley alone to hurriedly check the sheet and make sure she was completely covered. She had already embarrassed herself once this afternoon by clinging to Hunter, sobbing on his shoulder as he carried her to his truck. Thankfully, he had been understanding—one more thing about him that didn't add up. It bothered her to think how much comfort she had found in his muscled arms. And here she was needing his strength and support again, but that didn't mean she trusted him. Now wasn't the time to analyze her reaction to him.

She pressed her splayed fingers over her abdomen, knowing she would do anything to keep her child safe for as long as possible. "Please, please be all right."

The door opened, and Dr. Rollins entered, followed by Hunter who looked anxious and a little pale despite his tan. He crossed the room in three steps and placed his hand on her arm. His discerning gaze took in every detail, including the paper gown that had slipped off her shoulder. "What have they told you?"

"Hang on, Dad," Dr. Rollins said. "We'll talk in just a minute. Why don't you go to the head of the table behind Mom and let's see if we can tell what's going on in there."

Hunter's serious expression reflected his concern. Finally, he circled the table, careful to not bump anything, and stood near her head.

Though he made her feel anxious and restless, she couldn't ignore the comfort and peace of mind his presence also brought, a fact that didn't please her. Tomorrow she would deal with her feelings, but not today, not when she needed him so.

Hunter scanned the room. From the look on his face, he had never been in an ob-gyn examining room where pictures hung on the ceiling instead of the walls. Had the circumstances been different, his expression would have made her laugh.

Dr. Rollins draped a second sheet over her and adjusted it to expose her abdomen. That done, he turned the dials on a computer screen before squirting a clear gel on her stomach.

Ashley jumped and sucked in a quick breath.

"What's wrong?" Hunter demanded, leaning over her, his palms cupping her face.

"The gel," she explained. "It's cold."

"Oh." The lines of tension bracketing his mouth eased.

"Sorry. I should have warned you." Dr. Rollins took what looked like a wand and rolled it across her stomach, going in circles as if homing in on something.

Hunter looked from the screen to her stomach and back, and Ashley couldn't help but wonder if he was even half as scared as she. His features might as well have been carved from stone, giving no hint of what he thought or felt.

Every now and then her doctor paused to push a button or adjust a dial. "There, do you see him?"

"Him?" She saw a tiny image, proof positive that she was indeed pregnant, then couldn't see anything for the sudden tears of joy that sprang to her eyes. Her heart swelled to bursting with a mother's love for the baby nestled inside her.

"It could be a her," Dr. Rollins said with a shrug. "It's too soon to tell the sex by looking." He checked her chart. "In another two weeks, we should be able to hear the heartbeat."

Hunter leaned over the table, squinting at the screen. "Looks like a peanut. Or am I looking at the wrong thing?"

It did look like a peanut, a precious peanut, though Ashley would never admit it to him.

Dr. Rollins pointed to a light shape on the screen. "I think I see the problem. There's another one."

Ashley's heart galloped as she scrubbed the tears from her eyes with the heels of her hands and blinked several times.

"Another one what?" Hunter asked.

Ashley wasn't sure who grabbed who, only that their hands were now clasped tightly together.

"Yes, I'm sure of it. Look, you can see both of them. You've got a pair. Twins." Dr. Rollins pushed another button and pulled a sheet of dark paper from the side of the machine.

"Twins?" Hunter asked.

"Just two?" Ashley couldn't bear the thought that the third egg hadn't survived the procedure.

Hunter frowned. "What do you mean 'just two'? How many eggs did you have implanted, anyway?"

Her heart beat out a rapid tempo. "Three."

"Three?" he hissed. "What were you thinking?"

Dr. Rollins gave them both a questioning look before turning his attention back to the computer screen.

Ashley had known there were drawbacks to multiple births, but she'd only had three eggs left and enough money to have one last in vitro procedure. She had decided to go for broke and didn't regret her decision, would never regret it no matter what she had to endure. "I wanted a baby so badly, I was willing to take a chance that all three might make it."

He released her hands and dried her tears with the pads of his thumbs. "Well, it looks as if we've got two."

She gave him a searching look and saw the concern in his eyes and something else she couldn't understand. Before, there had only been her. Now, suddenly, Hunter had brought "we" into the mix. Unsure how she felt about his presumption, she grudgingly admitted he was the father of her babies. He had been so kind to her today, proving he wasn't as unfeeling as she'd originally thought, but how much was she willing to concede? Not that this was the time to think about it. For now her only concern was the health of her babies.

"Hunter, this is more than you bargained for. I want you to know I assume total responsibility for these babies."

"Not anymore."

"What do you mean?"

He raked a hand through his normally immaculate black hair. "I don't know what I mean, exactly. Just that I'll do the right thing. You won't go through this alone."

She experienced déjà vu. A tremor spiraled up her spine. Her ex-husband had made much the same promise when they'd learned blocked fallopian tubes prevented her from conceiving in the traditional manner. She had been naive and believed him. Later she had discovered that while she'd been poked and probed, taken shots and done everything possible to conceive, he had been having an affair with his secretary. Never again. "I won't be alone. I've got my babies."

"Well, now you've got me, too." Hunter shifted his attention to Dr. Rollins who had turned his chair away to write notes in a chart, giving them a measure of privacy. "So, Doc, do you see any more hiding in there?"

The doctor swivelled to face them. "It's hard to tell at this stage, but no, I don't think so."

"Are the two remaining babies okay?" Ashley asked, biting her bottom lip to keep it from trembling. She almost hadn't asked for fear of what he might say, but she had to know.

Her doctor pushed the equipment away and swiped a towel over her stomach to remove the gel. "I don't see anything unusual."

"What about the bleeding?" Hunter asked. "Is the third egg that didn't make it in any way connected with that?"

"I don't think so. Ashley's a small woman. Anytime you have multiple births, the risks double or triple. So, here's what we'll do. I want you to see that your wife takes it easy."

"She's not my—"

"What about my job?" Ashley asked, interrupting whatever Hunter had been about to say. Anxiety knotted her stomach.

"What kind of work do you do?" Dr. Rollins asked.

"I'm a legal secretary."

"Last night she worked till nine," Hunter said. "Knowing her boss, stressful is an understatement."

Ashley wished Hunter would hush. "It isn't that bad."

Dr. Rollins looked at her, his expression serious. "With multiple births, the chance of early delivery is a certainty, and you're already having problems. If you want these babies to have a fighting chance, you're going to have to be truthful with me."

She didn't have to think about her decision, because she would make any sacrifice for her babies. "All right."

"Are you under a lot of stress at work?" the doctor asked.

Hunter squeezed her shoulder.

His touch distracted her so much she had to close her eyes for a minute and think before she could answer. "Yes."

"Do you work a lot of extra hours?"

"Yes."

Dr. Rollins made a note in his chart, then set it aside. "I know this will be difficult, but I wouldn't recommend it if I didn't think it absolutely necessary."

Ashley could only nod and blink away the threat of new tears. Her pulse raced, and a wave of dizziness came upon her, then left just as suddenly.

"Some women spot their entire pregnancy, though we prefer that they not. Until we see what you're going to do, I'm classifying you as high risk. That means no driving, no shopping, no working." Dr. Rollins looked from her to Hunter. "Dad, I want her off her feet. You do the cooking and laundry or hire someone to do it, but I want her in bed for two weeks, a month or however long it takes to get this bleeding stopped. After that, she can get up and putter around the house for maybe an hour at a time, then go back to bed for a couple of hours. No lifting. No cleaning. Nothing at all for at least two weeks. Then, as long as she's doing okay and not bleeding, she can go back to work, but only part-time. And I'll want to see her before she resumes working. We're going to take this one day at a time."

"I'll see that she follows your instructions," Hunter said.

Their voices seemed to come to Ashley from far away. She had never thought beyond the conception, refused to believe there might be complications with her pregnancy. Now she realized the extent of her foolishness. She might have finally conceived only to miscarry.

Getting off work for two weeks when they were so busy would be difficult. But she would find a way. She had no choice.

Because she couldn't face even one tomorrow without her precious babies.

# *Chapter Four*

"I appreciate you taking me to see Dr. Rollins and staying with me, but I'm fine now."

Hunter followed Ashley into her apartment. "You and I have some unfinished business, that is if you're feeling up to it." While waiting for her to dress at the doctor's office, he had called work and had them clear his schedule for the following day. Something he had never done...until Ashley.

She threw up her hands and shoved the door shut. "Unfinished business. No, I don't think so."

He strode into the living room and moved the partially packed suitcase from the sofa. "I think we both know better than that. Why don't you lay down?"

"Look, Hunter—"

"The doctor said to keep you in bed and that's what I intend to do." Seeing his children on the ultrasound screen had suddenly made the situation with him and Ashley very, very real, and though he wanted to hold her, they needed to talk.

Color rose to her cheeks. "Oh."

"Where can I get you a blanket?"

"In my bedroom closet."

When she continued to stand, he gave her a pointed look and gestured at the couch before going in search of a blanket. He entered her bedroom, the scent of vanilla growing stronger. Hunter didn't know what he had expected, but it wasn't this old-fashioned bedroom with a double bed, centered on one wall, draped with a cream crocheted spread. A book lay open in a rocking chair beside a round table and lamp.

Hunter lifted the paperback and examined the cover. *The First Few Months of Pregnancy*. He remembered the feel of her tummy beneath his palm and smiled, returning the book to the chair.

Turning, he opened the closet door. Three pairs of shoes sat in perfect alignment on the floor. A couple of dresses, blouses, slacks and skirts filled half the closet. The rest stood empty. Glancing up, he saw two blankets and grabbed one.

His mother had always said a woman's closet revealed her deepest secrets. He hadn't understood it until now and glanced inside again before closing the doors. It felt almost barren. The few things there revealed a frugal lifestyle. He saw no knickknacks women liked to collect or shoes purchased on sale which invariably ended up cluttering the bottom of a closet.

He closed the doors, wondering what Ashley would do now, how she would get by, when it seemed obvious, at least to him, that she already had to pinch every penny twice.

Hunter returned to the living room and spread the cover over Ashley who had stretched out on the sofa. He settled in a chair across from her, his hands clasped between his parted knees, thinking of what he wanted to say, choosing his words carefully.

Finally he met her gaze and was almost thankful for the wariness in her brown eyes. He had a reputation for terrorizing his opponents, not that he wanted to do that now with Ashley. He also had a rebellious past to live down, but with any luck, she would never learn about that. Otherwise, she might not let him close to her or his children. He didn't want to upset her, but would make his point. He could only hope she would listen.

Hunter nodded toward the suitcase he had moved to the floor. "Going on a trip?"

"Trip?" She glanced at the bag he had indicated. "I packed that in case I had to stay in the hospital."

"You didn't take it with you."

"Because you came in like a Neanderthal and carted me off. Despite what you think, I wasn't running. That's not my style."

"So what exactly are your plans?" he asked, reading her tension when she picked at the balls of lint on the blanket.

"I don't know now. I thought I had it all planned out, but I never considered...I need more time to think about it."

"Do you have any family who can help out?"

"No."

"A distant relative?" he asked.

"No."

"A boyfriend?"

Her chin jutted forward in a stubborn manner he was coming to recognize. "That is none of your business."

"Under the circumstances, it is very much my business."

She sighed. "There's no one."

He fought the urge to smile and decided to ignore his

reaction to learning she had no one special in her life. "What about money?"

"I really don't see—"

"I'm trying to help you," he said.

"I didn't ask for your help."

"I know but I'm offering it, anyway. Do you have any savings or CDs?"

She clasped her hands in her lap. "Sort of."

"What does that mean?"

"The divorce. I was awarded forty thousand dollars. I've received half and will get the other half in four annual payments beginning in one year when my—when Kevin receives his annual bonus from the firm where he works."

It was obvious she felt uncomfortable talking about her ex-husband, and, frankly, Hunter didn't want to hear about him. "How much of the first half do you have left?"

She chewed her bottom lip. "A couple of thousand."

Had he been all wrong in his opinion of her? Had she squandered the settlement money on foolishness? "What happened to the rest?"

She looked at him, her eyes sparkling with challenge. "I had moving expenses, apartment and utility deposits and car insurance. Would you like a bill of costs, counselor?"

He did mental calculations and frowned. "No way would that total twenty thousand."

"And there was the in vitro. It was thirteen thousand."

He leaned toward her, not believing what he'd heard. "Thirteen thousand dollars?"

"No, Hunter, pesos." Ashley rolled her eyes. "I don't know why you're carrying on so. It's my money to do with as I please. I have a job. I was making it just fine, until this happened.

"I would have done it for free."

"Pardon?"

"I said I would have done it—"

"I heard you," she blurted out in a rush, color flooding her cheeks. "I wasn't sure I'd heard you correctly. But it wouldn't have worked."

"*It* works just fine."

He hadn't thought her face could get any redder, but it did. "That's not what I meant. I've got blocked fallopian tubes, so even if you had done *that* for free, it wouldn't have mattered."

He felt like a jerk because he hadn't considered why she couldn't get pregnant. "I'm sorry," he said, meaning it. She had stared at something over his left shoulder while telling him. Obviously, she believed this medical condition had left her somehow lacking. If anything, learning why she'd had the insemination made his opinion of her go up. Not many women would endure all that she had to have a child. Even though she believed doing *that* wouldn't have worked, the very idea had raised Hunter's awareness. As well as other things. Things that had nothing at all to do with their current situation. Things he'd be better off not thinking about.

"Just because you have a medical condition that makes conceiving difficult, doesn't mean you're in any way inferior. My brother has a low sperm count."

"I remember you telling me that. I couldn't understand why you would donate your sperm if you feel so strongly about being involved in your child's life."

Hunter tugged the blanket down to cover Ashley's feet. "For as long as I can remember, I've looked up to my older brother. Everything always seemed to come so easy to him. I, on the other hand, always seemed to be in trouble because of one thing or another. He ran interception between me and my folks. When I'd miss curfew, Jared would cover for me and leave our bedroom window open so I could climb inside without getting caught." Hunter realized he was spilling his guts and wondered what it was about Ashley that made him open up and talk about things he'd never shared with anyone else.

"Sounds like you two have a special relationship," Ashley said, drawing Hunter back to the present.

"We do. We're not as close as we used to be, but things changed after I was sent off to school. Now Jared's married and well, it's different. Even though I wouldn't have had a father-son relationship with the child if Lauren's insemination had resulted in a baby, I couldn't walk away from Jared when he needed me. Not when he had always been there for me." Not when Hunter had a chance to stop the anguish his brother felt at not having a child.

"I always wanted a sister or brother," Ashley said, "but it was just me."

So there really was no one else to come to her aid, except her ex-husband. It irked Hunter to think of her having to ask anyone other than him for help. Especially when the man in question was more than likely the one who had made her feel not good enough. But this wasn't about Hunter and what he wanted. If he was going to help her, he needed to know where she stood financially. "Ashley, is there any chance your ex could pay you the other half in one lump sum?"

"I don't think so. He married his secretary. I heard she has put him in debt up to his law degree."

"A lawyer?"

"Yeah. He practices with a large firm in Austin."

Hunter stored that information away as he stood and paced. "I don't see that either of us has much choice."

"I don't understand," she said, pushing herself to a sitting position on the couch.

"You're going to have to move in with me."

* * *

"No way am I moving in with you." Ashley threw the blanket to the back of the sofa. She hoped she had misunderstood what Hunter had just said.

She stood and tried to step around the end of the couch, but Hunter blocked her escape. "Will you listen to reason? These are my children. It's my duty to help you."

"You know, Hunter, I don't know what it is about men and duty, but I am sick to death of being told what to do." Ashley jabbed her index finger into his chest and took a step forward.

He glanced down at her finger making an indentation in his tie. "I'm thinking of you and the babies."

"You need to remember they're my babies, too," she said with a lift of her chin. "Possession is nine-tenths of the law."

One corner of his mouth twitched. "You've got me there."

Ashley realized what she'd said and laughed.

He squeezed her shoulders. "Remember what the doctor said about staying in bed." With gentle hands, Hunter helped her to settle on the sofa once more and covered her with the blanket, then he dragged a chair beside the sofa and sat down. "We need to talk about this."

Ashley turned on her side to face him and tucked her arm beneath her head. "It's really not necessary."

"Why not?" he asked, leaning forward with his elbows on his knees, his fingers entwined. "You're not afraid of me, are you?"

"Afraid? I was never—" The look he gave her stopped the denial she'd been about to voice. "Okay, I was a little intimidated by you before, but not anymore."

"Good." He studied her for a minute, making her uncomfortable with the intensity of his gaze. "Why don't you think staying with me is necessary?"

"We're only talking about two weeks. After that, assuming everything goes okay, I'll be back at work."

"The doctor said maybe even a month and after that he wants you working only part-time. That means you'll have to get by on half the money you're used to."

Ashley considered that a moment. "What I have in the bank along with my paycheck should be enough if I'm careful."

Hunter shoved his fingers through his hair, a telling action she had come to recognize as something he did when frustrated. "There's no reason to deplete your funds when I'm willing to—"

"Hunter," she reached out and placed her hand on his knee. "Arguing won't get us anywhere."

He studied her a minute. "You're right."

"I am?" she asked, surprised he had agreed.

"Yeah. We need to join forces."

"What do you mean?"

When she tried to withdraw her hand, he caught it between his. "Our focus should be on keeping our babies healthy. Instead of arguing, we should be using our combined energies to ensure that they stay where they are for as long as possible."

She tried to ignore the feel of his hands against hers. "How do you propose we do that?"

"Move in with me. Let me take care of you."

The way Hunter's touch had her insides quivering, she wasn't at all sure living with him was a good idea. "I don't know."

"Having you at my place won't cost me any extra, but think of what you'll save in rent and utilities."

"Maybe a thousand a month," she admitted.

"The doctor has already warned us multiple births can bring complications. Even if all goes well, and I hope it does, your expenses after the babies are born will be double what you expected. You're going to need every cent you have saved and probably then some. I confess I don't like the idea of you having to depend on your ex. What will you do if he doesn't come through with the next installment? Is he reliable? And even if he is, how long do you think you and two babies can live on the four annual installments of five thousand dollars each?''

When she didn't answer, he continued, ''I figured as much. Staying with me will accomplish two things. It will let you save your money for use later.''

''What's the other thing?'' she asked, amazed at how he attacked everything with logic.

''I'll be there to help.''

Ashley stared at his hands still holding hers. His touch distracted her, but it also warmed and comforted her, as his presence had done earlier in Dr. Rollins's office. Still, the enormity of everything that had happened this past week overwhelmed and frightened her.

Hunter released her hand and pulled a picture from inside his shirt pocket. He studied it a minute. His features softened, and he smiled before giving it to her. ''The nurse brought this out while you were dressing.''

Ashley took the black-and-white photo, a duplicate of what they'd seen on the ultrasound screen. Their babies. She blinked away the sudden tears that blurred her vision. ''I never stopped to consider what would happen if I conceived. After years of undergoing testing and different procedures and one failed in vitro, I had almost given up. I honestly didn't think I would ever conceive.''

''But you did,'' Hunter said.

''I wanted a baby so badly, I focused only on that. I didn't think about anything else.'' Knowing why she now found herself unprepared didn't relieve her guilt. ''I would never knowingly put a child of mine at risk, but that's what I've done.''

"You can't undo what happened yesterday or the day before, but you can change tomorrow." Hunter brushed a strand of hair from her temple. "From now on, there is no more you or me. It's all about our babies and what's best for them."

"I want to do what's right." Now her decisions affected so much more than just her. "But I'm so afraid I'll do the wrong thing."

"We've both made mistakes. I'm willing to go the distance with you to give our children a fighting chance. But I can't do it alone. And neither can you. Trust me, Ashley, to do what's best for you and our babies. Move in with me." He offered his hand.

She glanced once more at the ultrasound picture. They were so tiny. So helpless. So dependent on her to do the right thing. But what was that? Her ex-husband had made trusting another man almost impossible. Still, she could see the wisdom in Hunter's words. Moving in with him didn't have to mean surrendering control. Or trusting him.

Ashley transferred the picture to her left hand and placed her right in Hunter's. "You, Mr. Prosecutor, have got yourself a roommate."

The twin grooves bracketing his mouth deepened as he watched her for a long moment, almost as if giving her time to change her mind. "Are you sure? Once we do this, there's no going back."

How could she be positive? Past certainties had ended in betrayal, leaving her shattered and alone. This time she would put her babies first. She'd made the decision to move in with Hunter with her eyes wide open and wouldn't be blinded by a handsome face. "Yes, I'm sure."

The following Sunday evening, Hunter stood beside the couch for a long moment watching Ashley sleep. Moving day had been harder on her than he'd realized. She had wanted to go with him to take the last of her things to his house, but after loading her bed and clothes, there hadn't been room for her in his truck. So he'd left her behind to rest. Seeing how soundly she slept, he hated to wake her.

Now, with no one to witness his transgression, he looked his fill. Petite, but such a fighter. His gaze moved leisurely over her freckled nose, stubborn chin and lips that twitched in her sleep as if to smile. If anyone deserved to smile, she did. She was a good woman, the mother of his children, and he intended to do everything in his power to give her a reason to smile again. He didn't know much about pregnancy and what to expect in the coming months, but he would do his best to make her happy and keep her safe.

Hunter leaned over Ashley and lifted the book from her abdomen. He had thought to slide his arms beneath her back and legs and lift her, but his gaze locked on her stomach where his children grew.

*Children.* A burning need to protect burst inside him like an exploding Roman candle on the Fourth of July. A week ago, his only concern had been getting bad guys off the street and hoping Lauren conceived. Now he was a father-in-waiting to two babies.

Hunter couldn't help but wonder if they would both be girls or boys or one of each. Not that it mattered. He would love them no matter what. Truth be known, he already did. Whatever the future might bring, they would grow up knowing his love.

First, he had to take care of Ashley, do everything possible to see that their babies stayed where they were until it was safe for them to be born. But how long was that? Had the doctor told Ashley her due date? Glancing at the book in his hand, he perched on the edge of the sofa, settled his elbows on his knees and began to read.

"Hunter?"

He glanced over to find Ashley watching him. Sleep had

left her soft and desirable, warm and willing, and the urge to protect her came swift and hard like a guilty verdict. The only thing that stopped him from pulling her into his arms was sleep had also exposed her trusting nature and vulnerability. Responsibility went with his job and he'd always shouldered it with ease, until now. He had asked Ashley to trust him and he needed to prove himself worthy, something he hadn't always been. With his frustration barely in check, he said, "Let's go home."

"Home?" she asked.

Funny how the words had rolled so easily off his tongue as if the phrase was something he used often. To him, his house and land outside of town were an investment and a place to live. Nothing more. "I want you to think of my place as your home."

She wet her lips with the tip of her tongue. "I hope we're not making a mistake."

He stilled at her words. "Do you think we are?"

"I honestly don't know. I wish I did."

Hunter handed her the book and helped her to stand, keeping her close to his side. "I understand how you must feel, giving up your apartment and moving in with me. If I was renting, I would have let my place go and stayed with you. Since I'm buying my house and it's larger, we made the logical choice."

"I know, and I appreciate everything you've done."

He sensed there was more. "But?"

"There's still so much that could go wrong."

Hunter knew all about doing wrong, but the subtle scent of vanilla kept him from dwelling on it. "Such as?"

"My boss finding out, for one. If he learns we're living together, I'll lose my job."

Hunter didn't see that as a great loss. Williams was a class "A" jerk. "There are other jobs, better jobs where you will be appreciated and won't be worked to death, but that's not something we need to consider now. First, we have to get the bleeding under control. After the doctor says it's okay, you can go back to work part-time. Do you want me to call Williams tomorrow morning and explain everything?"

"No, I'll do it." She tipped her head back to look at him. "You don't think very highly of my boss, do you?"

He arched a brow. "Does it show?"

"Only a little. I know he's a prima donna at times, but I like what I do. Besides, it pays the rent."

Hunter grew serious and met her gaze. "You don't pay rent anymore. That's my job now."

"Well, yes," she said, "but once—"

"No, Ashley. Remember, one day at a time."

She gave him a wobbly smile. "Okay."

"From now on, I'll do all the worrying. Your only job is to take good care of my children."

*"Our children."*

Hunter laughed as he closed and locked her apartment door. "Are you one of those females who always has to have the last word?"

She looked at him with feigned innocence. "Who me?"

The tremor that snaked down his spine wasn't caused by the cold North Texas afternoon. He held her close to his side as they walked down the stairs and to his truck. He tried to ignore the way she felt pressed against him, but failed. Again, he wondered why this particular woman affected him so and how he was supposed to live in the same house with her without going nuts.

# Chapter Five

Ashley didn't know what kind of house she had expected, but it wasn't a large Victorian-looking farm house. To the left of the main structure stood a barn, bleached to a pale grayish red by age and the Texas sun. One door hung at an angle. The other was gone.

She noticed a tiny building barely visible some distance behind the home. It leaned a little to one side and had a crescent moon cut in the top of the door. It looked like a child's playhouse, only taller. "Is that what I think it is?"

Hunter opened the truck's passenger door and circled his palms around Ashley's waist to help her out. "It's an outhouse."

"You don't have indoor plumbing?"

"Why, are you worried you'll have to tiptoe barefoot through the early morning dew?"

The idea of kicking off her shoes and drawing air free of exhaust fumes into her lungs made her smile. Birds chirped in the nearby trees, a refreshing change from the blaring music, screeching brakes and honking horns she'd grown accustomed to hearing. "I'd do it. Since I left for college the only grass I've known up close and personal grew in parking lot cracks."

His expression softened. "You can walk all you want…as long as the doctor says it's okay, but don't explore alone."

"Why not?"

"I don't want you wandering off without me."

Surely he didn't expect to keep her under lock and key. She really should have considered the consequences of living with a man she knew very little about. "Before I agreed to stay with you, I probably should have asked what expectations you had."

"Expectations?"

Ashley cleared her throat, aware that Hunter's hands still rested at her waist. "I mean you're a man, and I'm a woman."

"Really? I hadn't noticed."

"You're not going to make this easy, are you?"

"No." Laughter shone in his blue eyes. "I don't have any expectations, so you can relax."

Hunter glanced at the large black dog that barked as it rounded the corner of the house at a run. "That's Sheeba. She's a chow and lab mix and the best-tempered dog you'll ever find."

He squatted as Sheeba neared, and then patted her. The dog's head resembled a bear's and the tongue that hung from her mouth was black. Her long hair made her look like a sheep.

Sheeba circled to Ashley who petted her. The dog sniffed her hand, then nuzzled it and wagged her thick tail that curled over her back. "Doesn't she get hot during the summer?"

"Yeah, but there's a stock tank out back. When she's not aggravating the cats or chasing a rabbit, she's in it."

"You have cats, too?"

"Yeah, they stay in the barn or under the house. Come on, you need to get off your feet."

When he took her hand and started toward the house, she pulled back to glance at the open pastures surrounding them.

He turned to face her. "Do you need my help?"

"You're acting like I'm an invalid. I promise I'm more than capable of walking to the house."

Hunter gave her a skeptical look, but finally released her. He walked by her side as they moved from his truck. When she started up the steps onto the porch, he gripped her elbow.

"Hunter."

He opened the screen door and slipped his key into the deadbolt, then looked at her. "Yes."

"I'm a big girl. I can go exploring without getting lost."

"You have a good sense of direction?"

"Yes."

"How do you feel about snakes?"

"Snakes?" *Dear Lord.* What had she gotten herself into? "Is it too late to change my mind about staying?"

"Yeah. I don't want you taking any risks until I have a chance to get out back and mow all the tall grass. Or is it something else that has you wanting to hightail it out of here?" He frowned then, deepening the creases at the corners of his eyes. "I know this place doesn't look like much from the outside, but I think you'll be comfortable. I've focused on remodeling the inside since I bought it and had planned to paint the house and barn when it warms up in the spring."

Ashley hadn't thought him the type to do what her ex

had considered menial labor. Everything she'd learned about Hunter since the day he'd announced he was the father of her children was in direct opposition to what she had believed of him. Her reluctance to stay had come with the realization of how little she knew about the man with whom she would be living. Still it sounded as if he thought her a snob. "Do you think something as insignificant as a coat of paint would keep me from staying?"

He studied her a minute. "No, I guess not," he said as he turned the key and pushed open the door.

Hunter flipped on the light switch as he stepped inside behind Ashley and shut the door. Polished wood floors gleamed beneath the overhead wagon wheel chandelier. The sight robbed Ashley of the ability to speak.

She felt as if she had been transported to another era. She gazed around the room, taking in the large area rug beneath a wooden coffee table. Behind it sat a tan sectional sofa. On the wall behind the couch were two paintings of cowboys on horseback, and underneath a window sat a butter churn that gave a touch of family warmth to the room.

Hunter directed her past the staircase and down a hallway until they came to a closed door he identified as his room. Without letting her see inside, he pointed out a room next to his where he had put her bed. After that he rushed her past the bathroom and into the kitchen. He opened a door she thought was a pantry, but instead she saw stairs that went down.

"I don't want you going in the basement."

"Snakes?"

"No, killer steps. They're old and rickety. I'm afraid you'll fall. There's nothing of interest down there, except a few power tools." Hunter closed the door, then accompanied her back into the living room to a beautiful staircase.

"These lead to the second story, and then above that

there's an attic. I've got everything up there closed off since I haven't worked beyond this floor. I'm still a long way from done, but I'm making progress.''

"This isn't at all what I'd expected," she admitted, moving to run her hand up the polished wooden banister.

"Really? What did you think I'd live in, a hovel?" he asked, his voice filled with challenge.

"No." She gave him a teasing grin. "Whenever you marched into our offices, you always wore a starched shirt, dark suit, and a frown. Based on your reputation, you're very successful."

"So you expected manicured lawns in a highbrow neighborhood? You have me confused with my father."

She remained silent, not believing what she'd admitted or his response. "Hunter, I— That was before—" She sighed. "All I meant is that this isn't what I'd expected."

Hunter stepped closer until he blocked everything else from view and she had no choice but to look up at him. "Don't be afraid to say what you think. If this is going to work between us, we have to be honest with each other, even when it's tough."

"All right." She wondered if he had meant what he'd said.

The intensity of his blue eyes made it difficult to concentrate, especially when surrounded by the heady aroma of new wood, soft leather and Hunter.

"So, what do you really think?" He moved closer.

She thought she was in big trouble. "About?"

"The house, at least what you've seen."

She turned away from him, confused by the way her heart raced whenever he was near. With a quick glance around the room, she said, "You should be very proud of what you've done. I felt welcome as soon as we came through the door. It conveys an inviting comfort. It feels like home." Something she hadn't had in a very long time. She closed her eyes, wanting to shut out the painful memories that followed.

Hunter cursed under his breath, lifted her in his arms and carried her to the couch. "I let you do too much."

"Bull. I've done nothing all weekend but give orders, and you made me do that from the sofa. I don't feel bad, really. Honestly, Hunter, please put me down."

He watched her closely. "Then what's wrong? You looked as if you were hurting."

She was hurting, but not in the way he thought. "The staircase reminded me of when I was little. Our house was big and old like this one. We didn't have much money, but we had a whole lot of love."

"Do your folks live in Texas?"

"They did until my freshman year in college when they were killed in a car wreck."

Hunter lowered her onto the couch and sat on the edge. "I'm sorry. I didn't know."

Ashley hadn't shared much of her past with anyone, but she figured that the father of her children had a right to know. "It's been years. I should be used to them being gone, but I'm not. Sometimes, like now, I'll see something that triggers a memory and it's like losing them all over again."

"You don't have any other family?"

"No. You mentioned a brother. Does he live in Hale?"

Hunter pushed to his feet and crossed the room to look out a window. "Jared and his wife and my parents live in town. Jared and Buck have a law office in that new bank building across town."

Until Hunter had invited himself into her life, she had planned to raise her child by herself, but after the recent scare she no longer wanted to be alone. If anything happened to her like it had her parents, she wanted her children to have someone strong to take care of them, someone like Hunter. "You're very lucky to live so close to your family. At least our babies will have one set of grandparents and an aunt and uncle." *And they'll have a loving father with whom to share the many joys of life.*

He braced his hands on either side of the window and leaned his forehead against one bicep. "I haven't told my folks."

"But you do plan to, don't you? With my parents already gone, that only leaves yours. You have to tell them."

"I don't know." He turned and made his way to the end of the couch. "I'm not saying anything to anyone until I figure out how to break the news to my brother."

"Jared?"

"Yeah. After this last insemination attempt failed, Jared and his wife decided to stop trying for a while. I can only imagine what hearing about this will do to them."

"I'm sorry. I know how painful it is to go through the shots, praying the whole time, trying not to get your hopes up, but doing it anyway. You're right to consider their feelings. I'm sorry if I've put you in a difficult position. If you'd like, we could have them over one night and tell them then."

"No. I'll take my brother off somewhere—just me and him. I haven't figured out how I can tell him I'm going to be a father when he's really the one who deserves to have a child." Hunter strode toward the kitchen.

His blatant rejection of her offer was like a slap in the face. He'd made it abundantly clear that she wasn't a part of his family. She tried not to let it get to her, but it did. "Hunter," she said, her words bringing him to a stop. "What about your folks? What if you told them first so they could be there for moral support when you talk to Jared?''

He had paused in the doorway, his back still to her, his shoulders rigid. "You don't know my parents. This won't be news they'll welcome. My mom will come around after she gets over the initial shock, but things with my father are a little strained. I think it best if I tell Jared alone."

Ashley listened as Hunter's steps faded into the distance, followed by the slamming of the back door. His dread was as tangible as his making Ashley feel like an outsider, the same as her children would feel unless she brought about a change.

Hunter wouldn't like her interference, but she couldn't let his stubbornness stand in the way of her children having a family, something she missed terribly. With her carrying twins, she would likely be showing soon and their little secret would be out anyway. She would give him a reasonable period of time to break the news, then she would take matters into her own hands.

Ashley settled in her chair and flipped on her computer, glad to be back on the job, even if only part-time. The past two weeks had bored her to tears.

Her initial concern over living with Hunter had quickly evaporated. While she'd made friends with Sheeba and the cats, Hunter had spent all of his days and half of each night at the office preparing for a trial scheduled to start today.

On those few nights when they had shared dinner, she found herself drawn to the mystery behind the man. During those encounters, she'd sometimes get a glimpse of a different side of him that surprised and intrigued her. It seemed almost as if his prosecutor facade came off along with the pinstriped power suit. She preferred him in faded jeans even if the way they molded to his thighs did distract her. Because dressed in worn jeans and a T-shirt, Hunter was different. Handsome. Sexy. Charming. But more than that, he was almost vulnerable.

His frequent and all too brief calls to check on her had kept Ashley from going completely crazy. But now she had returned to work and judging from the stack of files on her desk, her days of boredom were at an end.

Sometime later Ashley pulled the deposition notice draft from her laser printer as the phone rang. "This is Ashley Morgen, may I help you."

"You're still there?" Hunter's voice was low, his statement civil, but she had talked with him enough the past two weeks to know *that* tone. He wasn't pleased.

In spite of that, his call lifted her spirits. "Well, yes. Am I supposed to be somewhere else?"

"The doctor didn't want you working past noon."

"But it's only," she glanced at her watch and gasped, "one o'clock. I guess I lost track of the time."

"You're ready to leave, right?"

"Just about. I only have a short tape left to transcribe that a client is picking up."

"What did Williams say when you told him?"

She didn't want to tell Hunter, but she didn't see any way around it. "I haven't told him yet."

"Why not?"

"It's not that easy."

"How hard can it be? You just walk into his office and say—"

"I know. I know. He was out of the office taking a deposition all morning. Every time I've tried to speak to him, he gets a call or someone interrupts. I've already filled out papers for personnel. I had hoped to be the one to tell him."

"Does he know why you took off the past two weeks?"

"No." Ashley sighed, worrying about the coming meeting with her boss. "I was afraid he would ask questions I wasn't prepared to answer, so I took vacation time I had coming."

"You won't be able to hide your pregnancy much longer."

"It's not the pregnancy I need to keep a secret, but you. Once he knows I'm carrying your children, he'll draw the wrong conclusion."

"What makes you think that?"

"He's made his position about me seeing you very clear. I don't want to risk losing my job until I absolutely have to."

"Maybe he'll surprise you."

"Maybe." But she doubted it.

"You sound tired. Are you okay?"

The concern in his voice made her smile. "Yeah. I've gotten lazy, that's all. How's your trial going?"

"We're not done picking a jury yet. Since voir dire has taken so long, I don't imagine we'll put on evidence today."

"Does that mean another late night?" she asked, admitting to herself she'd missed him.

"No. I'm beat. I'm looking forward to an evening at home. I need to review a video deposition, but that won't take long. How about I pick something up for dinner when I leave?"

"Sounds great," she said. And it did. Her anticipation came not from the food, but the idea of spending the evening with Hunter. Her hand froze over the envelope she'd been sealing. Odd she should want to be with *him*. She was obviously more lonely than she'd realized. On the verge of being totally desperate for his company.

"Listen," Hunter said, "the bailiff's motioning everyone

back inside the courtroom. I've got to run. Try to get out of there soon, okay?''

''I'll be gone in ten minutes max.''

''All right. I'll see you at the house.''

Ashley hung up and proofed a document before taking it in to Mr. Williams. She took a seat, intending to speak with him once he finished reviewing the pleading, but he was interrupted twice by incoming calls. Then an attorney dropped by to discuss a case. Giving up, she left his office and waited at her desk.

Ashley leaned her head on her folded arms, waiting for her boss's office door to open. She wanted to go home, could barely hold her eyes open, but needed to talk to Mr. Williams before leaving.

She glanced at her watch, then lowered her head again. *Three o'clock.* For the past two weeks, this had been nap time.

''Why are you still here?''

Her head snapped up at the sound of a familiar male voice. ''Hunter?''

He turned her swivel chair and leaned over her, his gaze assessing her with a thoroughness she found disconcerting. And maybe a little exciting. ''What's wrong?''

''What are you doing here?'' she asked.

''Are you all right?''

''Yes, of course. I'm fine.''

He didn't look as if he believed her. ''I saw your car outside. You should have left three hours ago.''

''I know. I've been trying to talk with Mr. Williams,'' she said, taking Hunter's arm, trying to maneuver him toward the door. ''You've got to go before someone sees you.''

He refused to budge. ''Not until you give me your word that you'll leave now.''

"Hunter," she hissed.

"Fine. I'll carry you to your car."

"Don't you dare." Her face grew hot with embarrassment and frustration. "I'm pregnant, not an invalid."

"Pregnant?"

The voice made Ashley turn, confirming her worst fear. Mr. Williams stood in the doorway.

Of all the people to walk into her office now and find the assistant D.A. leaning over her, why did it have to be her boss?

She knew how damning this looked. A million possible solutions raced through her mind, but none that seemed logical.

"Did you say pregnant?" Williams repeated.

Hunter stepped back as Ashley stood, his hand settling on her spine.

Ashley decided she might have to kill Hunter. As for her boss, she would do the only thing she could under the circumstances. Tell him the truth. Well, at least part of it. "I've tried to talk to you several times this morning, but we kept getting interrupted. I am pregnant." She tried to gauge his reaction to that news, then continued, "With twins. My doctor thinks it would be best if I work half days. I've already given the paperwork to personnel, and it's been approved."

Williams gave Hunter a challenging look. "What's your role in this?"

Hunter met her boss's glare. "I'm the father. Is that a problem?"

"You're damned right that's a problem." Williams pinned Ashley with a hard look. "I warned you about seeing him. You leave me no alternative but to fire you for breach of our firm confidentiality policy. Accounting will mail you a check for whatever you have coming."

Hunter took a step forward. "Williams, think about what you're saying. You're setting yourself up for a wrongful discharge suit."

Her boss looked as if he wanted to punch Hunter. "Don't tell me the law. Clear out of here before I call security."

"There's no reason to treat her like this," Hunter said. "From what I've seen, Ashley has worked late when you've asked and otherwise been a damned good employee."

A look of scorn twisted Williams's face. "This is one time you won't win. How does it feel?"

Hunter's hands fisted. "So this is about me and not her?"

Ashley decided the situation was slipping away from her, and she needed to regain control. "Mr. Williams, I need this job."

"You should have thought about that before sleeping with Morgan."

"But I didn't—"

"Ashley," Hunter said, gripping her arm, "don't waste your breath."

She shook off his hand, needing to make him understand how important this was to her. "I have to keep this job. I have nothing else."

"You've got me."

If the situation hadn't been so serious, she might have admired Hunter's chivalry. But she had just lost the only stability in her life. If only he had waited outside. "This isn't a game of one-upmanship. It's my life."

"We're in this together, remember. Where's your jacket?" The conviction in his tone touched a spot deep inside her.

"Behind the door." Ashley got her purse, unable to decide who she was angrier with, her boss or Hunter.

Hunter handed Ashley her coat and stepped past Williams into the hallway.

Ashley faced her boss. "I know you don't like Hunter, but you're all wrong about him and me."

Williams stuck out his hand, palm up. "Your office key."

She pulled the ring from her coat pocket and removed the front door key which she placed on his palm. Then she marched past Hunter and from her office.

Her steps faltered. Secretaries and attorneys filled the hallway. Whispered speculation of the events unfolding and her involvement with the prosecutor reached her.

Her face burned with humiliation. When Hunter tried to take her elbow, she pulled from his grasp. She wanted to yell, maybe even stomp her foot in frustration, but after another glance at the growing crowd, clamped her mouth shut. She tipped her chin up and strode toward the door. Finally, just when she thought she couldn't bear the curious stares and comments any longer, Hunter pushed open the front door and followed her outside.

She hurried down the sidewalk, unsure of her destination, knowing only that everything had been wrenched from her control. She was frightened. And now, she was also unemployed. It wasn't totally Hunter's fault, she admitted, but darn it, she needed to vent. And he was handy.

He came up behind her. "We'll leave your car here. I can get someone from my office to drop it by the house tomorrow."

She turned on him, intending to make a point. "I am not helpless. I have a mind, and I know how to use it."

"I never thought—"

"Yes, you did. You have from that first day when you walked into the conference room."

"If that's what I've done, I didn't realize it. I went looking for you because I was concerned. I wanted to make sure you were okay.''

"I appreciate that, but I'm a big girl." She dug in her pocket for her car keys. "I need to be alone for a while."

He gave her a doubting look. "You're pale and look like you could fall over at any minute. Let me take you home."

"I really don't—"

"Think of the babies, Ashley. Their safety. And yours."

He had her there, and she knew it. She hated it when he was right, especially now when all she wanted was to get away from him so she could think.

Without a word, she walked toward his truck, her mind a blur of hurt and betrayal. How had everything gotten so out of control? And why, after what had just happened, was she following him like a puppy?

She would let him drive her home because at this moment, she wasn't sure she had the strength to push in her car's clutch. But that was all she was willing to concede to him. Once home in her room, she would think everything through, then make her own decision—without regard to what Hunter Morgan wanted.

After Ashley had refused to respond to Hunter's two attempts at conversation, the ride home had been made in silence. But that hadn't stopped the tension that continued to build between them.

Throughout dinner, she'd felt his gaze on her, but had chosen to ignore him while thinking of everything that had happened. And now as she stood at the kitchen sink attacking the pan in time to the pounding of her head, Hunter sat behind her boring holes in her back as well as her resolve. In spite of that, Ashley felt she finally had a firm grip on her temper. Better to tell him tonight what she'd decided.

"I can't go on living here with things as they are. It won't work unless you stop trying to run my life." She gauged his reaction in the window over the kitchen sink.

His chair legs scraped across the shiny tile as he shoved it back and stood. "You know that's not what I'm doing."

How could he not see what was so clear? "Could have fooled me."

He cocked a hip against the counter beside her, his irritation palpable. "If you're referring to this afternoon, what would you have had me do?"

She took out her frustration on the bottom of the pan. "You shouldn't have come to the office."

"Ashley, I'm sorry about what happened, but Williams would eventually have found out about us."

When he touched her arm, she shook off his hand. "Yes, later, but at least I'd have had my job for a while longer."

"So you blame me?"

She blew out a loud breath as she grabbed the towel to dry her hands. "You stood up for me, and I appreciate that."

"But?"

"I wanted to pinch you for interfering. Under the circumstances, staying here isn't an option."

"Why not?"

"I don't think it will work anymore."

"The hell it won't. It's been working. You're just mad at me now, but once you get over—"

"Mad? Oh, that's rich." He hadn't seen mad yet. "Hunter, I went beyond being angry when you announced to my boss that you were the father of my children. Right now I'm furious with you."

"But I am the father, and getting mad won't change that. And why are you doing dishes?" Hunter took the towel from her and placed it on the counter.

"You're not listening. I have no job. No apartment. And talking to you is like talking to the wall. You're making me crazy."

Hunter's gaze lingered on her mouth. "The feeling is mutual, and I've had about all of this craziness I can stand." He slid his fingers around her nape and kissed her.

A roar filled her ears. When everything began to spin, she caught the front of his T-shirt and hung on for dear life. She thought to pull away, but when his tongue traced the seam of her lips, tempting and teasing her, she couldn't think at all.

Ashley opened to him like a blossom to the morning sun. He took immediate advantage, sweeping the inside of her mouth. She welcomed the burning heat of his lips, the feel of his hand on her back. The stroke of his tongue dissolved her anger, and she found herself wanting more, needing more. Moments earlier she had wanted to kill him. Now, she just wanted to tug him closer.

Hunter broke the kiss and swore as he pulled away.

She tried to slow her breath that came in ragged gasps and touched her fingertips to her lips. "Why did you do that?" she asked in a husky voice that didn't belong to her. And why had she let him? And worse, why had she liked it?

He walked to the table and gathered the remaining dishes, then joined her once more at the sink counter. "Aside from being on your feet when you're not supposed to be, you were working up a good head of steam. Getting upset can't be good for you."

"You did that to get me to be quiet? Hunter, are you insane? I can't believe you think you can just go around doing things like that whenever the mood strikes."

When he leaned toward her, she held up a hand to stop

him. "Don't even think about it. That was the most ridiculous—"

"You didn't like it?" He frowned as he settled his hip against the counter.

She remembered the muscled hardness her fingers had pressed against moments earlier. "What?"

"The kiss."

Ashley stared at him, wondering if this was some sort of strategy to confuse her. He seemed to be doing that a lot lately. "I have just lost my job, thanks to you, and all you're concerned about is what I thought of the way you, you—"

"Kiss."

She swallowed. Her gaze locked on his mouth. She tried to look away, but the memory of his lips on hers made it impossible. And darn it, she wanted him to kiss her again. "If you're hoping I'll feed your already overinflated ego by telling you how wonderful it was, then you're in for a big disappointment."

He smiled. "Wonderful?"

*Yes.* "No."

"I could do it again if you need—"

"You're not kissing me again just to prove a point."

Hunter took her hand, distracting her with the sensations prompted by his touch. "And that point would be?"

She wanted to close her eyes to shut out the sight of him so near, tempting her, making her ache to know the touch of his lips once more. But she couldn't. The challenge and unspoken promise in his gaze held her captive. He brushed his thumb over her hand, making her shiver. "Okay, I admit I liked it, but that's all I'm saying, so drop it."

His lips lifted in a satisfied smile. "Okay."

"I'm still mad at you." Ashley forced her gaze away from him so she could think.

How had she gotten herself into this mess? The decision to move in with him had been a logical one, or so it had seemed, but the kiss they'd just shared was anything but sensible.

Now she had no job and nowhere to stay, except with the father of her children—the man who had gotten her fired. The same man who had just given her *the kiss* of her life.

## Chapter Six

Judging from his brother's state of undress when he'd answered the door, Hunter had dropped by at a bad time. But there was no good time for what he'd come to say and he lowered himself onto the sofa to wait while Jared got himself together.

Hunter wanted to get it done and over with so the tightness in his chest would ease a little. Then he could get home to Ashley, the first woman in a long time to get under his skin. He had no one to blame but himself. It wasn't as if he'd planned to kiss her. It had been a spur-of-the-moment thing, a no-big-deal kiss meant to shock her out of being angry with him. It had been a shock all right, only he'd been the one surprised, because it had turned out to be a big deal. A really big deal. Because kissing her once hadn't been nearly enough. And kissing her again was all he'd thought about since then.

He should have left well enough alone and let her be mad. He deserved her anger, because he had known he should have stayed outside. But he'd been worried about her and not thinking straight, something that seemed to be happening with startling frequency where Ashley was concerned. Okay, so he'd screwed up. Nothing new there, except this time, Ashley had lost her job as a result. The fact that it was the mother of his children who would suffer the consequences of his actions had kept him awake last night. Well, that and thinking about the way Ashley had responded to his kiss.

A door opened at the end of the hall, drawing Hunter from his thoughts as Jared tromped into his living room. "So, what's so important it can't wait?"

Actually, he wished he could put it off, but after his secretary had asked about a rumor circulating about him and Ashley, he'd decided his time was up. A door opened down the hallway and Lauren soon joined Jared on the couch.

Hunter didn't want to upset Lauren. "Jared, could I speak with you outside?"

Jared dropped his arm from the back of the couch and settled it around his wife's shoulders. "You can talk freely. Lauren and I don't keep secrets."

Lauren scooted to the edge of the couch and stood. "If my being here makes Hunter uncomfortable, I don't mind going in the other room."

"But I mind." Jared tugged her onto his lap, then gave Hunter his attention. "So, what's up?"

Hunter wished there was another way to tell Jared and Lauren without hurting them. But there wasn't, so he blurted it out. "I'm going to be a father."

Jared's mouth dropped open, then snapped shut, his expression one of concern. "Should I congratulate you?"

Shock moved over Lauren's face and though tears filled her eyes, she remained composed. "What's wrong with you, Jared? Of course, we should congratulate him. Hunter, I didn't know you were seeing someone steady."

"I'm not." Feeling their anguish, Hunter leaned forward and clasped his hands. "Or at least I wasn't."

"So, who is she and how did all this come about?" Jared asked.

"Her name is Ashley Morgen." Hunter didn't want to add to their pain any more than was necessary. He decided the details of the insemination and how he and Ashley had come together really didn't matter, not when Jared's and Lauren's misery was so painfully obvious. "Neither one of us intended to get involved. It just happened."

Jared's hand lingered at Lauren's waist. "What does she do for a living?"

"She's a legal secretary, or at least she was until her boss fired her. Richard Williams believes Ashley's living with me and being pregnant with my babies is a conflict of interest."

"You're living together?" Jared exchanged a long look with Lauren. "Wait a minute. Did you say babies?"

"Yeah," Hunter said, torn between his own sudden pride and concern for his brother and sister-in-law.

Lauren gave him a wobbly smile that slipped as a tear fell. "I'm sorry, Hunter. I'm really happy for you. I believe everything happens for a reason. I just hope it will happen to us one day."

"It will, baby. It will." Jared gathered his wife close and kissed her temple. "What do you plan to do, Hunter?"

"I don't know yet."

"What about Mom and Dad? Do they know?"

"No."

"You need to tell them before someone else does."

With the speed of gossip, they would find out soon enough. "I know. I'm not looking forward to it."

Jared raked his fingers through his tousled hair. "Yeah, well, I don't envy you."

"We really are happy for you, Hunter," Lauren said, wiping the tears from her cheeks as she stood. "We'll have you over for dinner so we can meet her."

"Thanks. That would be great." Hunter pushed from the chair and headed for the door as Jared reached for Lauren.

He heard her broken sob as he closed the door, and the knot in his gut tightened. He wished there was something more he could do to ease the blow he had given them, but knew there wasn't. At least they had each other. He'd never known a more perfect couple, not that he knew many very well. Since his return to Hale after a ten-year absence during which he had finished college and law school and worked for a law firm, he hadn't had much of a social life. Except for attending obligatory county functions. Now, with the babies coming, he wouldn't have the luxury of dating, not that he'd met anyone who made him want to make the effort. From now on he guessed the only woman in his life would be Ashley. He smiled at the thought. Why not? It wasn't like either of them had anyone else.

If they had to spend the rest of their lives together, it would be nice if they could have what Jared and Lauren shared. But if they couldn't have that, then at least Hunter could do the right thing by marrying Ashley.

There wouldn't be love, but raising their children, giving them a solid foundation and happy home, would be enough. It was the best thing to do, the right thing. He suddenly felt good, better than he'd felt in quite a while.

Now, he had only to convince Ashley that he was a man who would make a good father and husband, and not the young boy who had failed the mother of his first child by not standing up to their parents.

*  *  *

Today had been the pits. Alone all day. Totally bored. Totally alone. At least Ashley had been until two hours earlier when Hunter had come home. Though still somewhat miffed at him, she had never been so glad to see anyone in her life.

She lay on the couch and pretended interest in a TV program, but instead watched him pace like a caged animal. In the year she'd worked for Mr. Williams, she had witnessed Hunter in action in their offices and in court. Never had she seen him this agitated.

"Is your trial not going well?" The stunned look on Hunter's face made it clear she'd surprised him. She'd shocked herself, too. She hadn't talked to him since he'd asked her to rate his kiss. If he only knew how much that kiss had shaken her. But, of course, Hunter didn't know, would never know.

"Does this mean you're not mad anymore?"

His ebony hair stuck out in all directions where he'd run his fingers through the thickness. She wanted to go to him and brush the dark strands back into place. Not a good idea if she intended to distance herself. She had never been one to stay mad long, and keeping to herself was getting harder each day. "I'm still upset over losing my job, but I've had all day to paint my toenails while I can still see my feet and to think about everything that happened with Mr. Williams."

"Painted your toenails, huh?" He gave her a crooked smile she felt all the way to her freshly painted toenails, exactly where his eyes went as he moved toward her.

"Nice," he said, cupping the heel of her left foot as he lifted it for his inspection. "Good color."

She couldn't form a word as he ran the pad of his thumb back and forth over her arch, eliciting a series of tremors that snaked up her spine. Finally she managed, "Thank you."

He lowered her foot to the arm of the couch and sat on the edge beside her. "So, what did you decide while painting your nails?"

"That you were right. My boss would have found out about you being the father eventually. Williams has always been a jerk. I guess I've just gotten used to him."

"That doesn't excuse his behavior."

"He's a lawyer. They're all full of themselves." Too late she realized what she'd said and to whom. "Sorry."

His gaze settled on her mouth, making her uncomfortable. "So you've clumped me with Williams and others like him?"

She couldn't stop her grin. "Maybe before all this happened between us. Now I'm not so sure. You've been so busy that we haven't had much time together, but your bringing me here to share your house isn't what I would have expected from you."

His eyes lifted to meet hers. "I guess I'll have to be happy with that, for now. I'm sorry I've been gone so much. I didn't stop to think how often you'd be left alone."

She warmed under his intense gaze and needed to change the subject. "So, how's your trial going?"

"Good."

His actions didn't reflect that. If not the trial, then what had him worried? "Who's the defense attorney?" she asked, noticing the lines of tension bracketing his mouth.

"Wade Baker, that new lawyer who moved here from Houston."

"Is he as good as I've heard?"

"Better." Hunter brushed a lock of hair behind her ear, his touch making her stomach take flight. "He's making me work for this one."

She fought the urge to turn her cheek into his palm as it grazed her skin. "You don't think you'll win?"

"I don't know. Right now it's anybody's guess."

His cologne, mixed with the scent of starched shirt and sensuality, filled her with an overpowering urge to move closer, touch him. "But you always win."

He smiled, his index finger blazing a trail from her ear down her cheek to her chin. Once again he stared at her mouth. "Do I?"

She swallowed hard. Her pulse raced. "Yes."

He braced his arm on the back of the couch as if to keep from touching her again.

"Is it Wade Baker's expertise that's got you distracted?" *Hunter* had Ashley distracted. She wanted to think of anything except how close he was and whether he might kiss her again. And how much she wanted him to do exactly that.

He turned his head toward her. "I didn't realize it was that obvious."

"You picked at your dinner and haven't spent five minutes with the work you brought home."

Hunter pushed off the couch and moved to the window. "It's not Wade or the case."

"Is it that high school boy I heard you talking about on the phone last night?"

"No. Greg Johnson is a bright kid but he is running with a rough crowd. He's headed for trouble, and I'm trying to stop him before it happens. But that's not what is bothering me."

She longed to go to him and ease the tension that made his back rigid, but thought it best if she remained where she was. "What is it then?"

He shrugged and braced his hands on either side of the window. "I don't want to worry you with my problems."

Concern finally drew Ashley to his side. She pressed her palm against the heat of his back. "Don't shut me out."

Hunter turned to frown at her. "Is that what you think?"

"It's what you're doing. I know that what you do is none of my business, but my ex-husband—"

"Don't compare me to him." He took hold of her arms and drew her forward until her breasts brushed his chest.

Ashley was stunned into silence by the fact that he sounded like a lover. A jealous lover. She tried to take a step back, but his hands held her in place. "I didn't realize I was doing that."

He released her and dropped his hands to his sides. "It's not your fault. I've got a lot on my mind. I didn't mean to take it out on you."

"I would like to help, Hunter. Maybe if you told me what's bothering you, we could talk about it."

He gave her a long, searching look, then said, "I think we should get married."

Ashley's brown eyes widened. Her mouth opened and closed several times.

Hunter wasn't at all pleased by her reaction. "Come on, Ashley. Say something. I didn't think it was that bad an idea."

She stared at him. "Is this a joke?"

"Is that what you think? That I would tease you when we're both in this up to our necks?"

She clasped her hands together in front of her until her knuckles turned white. "Honestly, I don't know what to think anymore. I never expected, never considered..."

"I hadn't either until recently." Until he'd realized how good doing things for Ashley made him feel. Just being with her made him happy. "But if you think about it, it makes sense."

She drew a deep breath. "I disagree."

Silhouette authors will refresh you

Silhouette ROMANCE® 1444
$3.50 U.S.
$3.99 CAN
M/V

# DIANA PALMER

## MERCENARY WOMAN
### SOLDIERS OF FORTUNE

We'd like to send you **2 FREE** books and a surprise gift to introduce you to Silhouette Romance®. Accept our special offer today and

## Get Ready for a totally Refreshing Experience!

## HOW TO QUALIFY:

1. With a coin, carefully scratch off the silver area on the card at right to see what we have for you—2 FREE BOOKS and a FREE GIFT—ALL YOURS! ALL FREE!

2. Send back the card and you'll receive two brand-new Silhouette Romance® novels. These books have a cover price of $3.99 each in the U.S. and $4.50 each in Canada, but they are yours to keep absolutely free!

3. There's no catch. You're under no obligation to buy anything. We charge nothing—ZERO—for your first shipment and you don't have to make any minimum number of purchases—not even one!

4. The fact is, thousands of readers enjoy receiving books by mail from the Silhouette Reader Service®. They enjoy the convenience of home delivery…they like getting the best new novels at discount prices, BEFORE they're available in stores…and they love their *Heart to Heart* subscriber newsletter featuring author news, horoscopes, recipes, book reviews and much more!

5. We hope that after receiving your free books you'll want to remain a subscriber. But the choice is yours—to continue or cancel, any time at all. So why not take us up on our invitation with no risk of any kind. You'll be glad you did!

# SPECIAL FREE GIFT!

We can't tell you what it is…but we're sure you'll like it! A FREE gift just for giving the Silhouette Reader Service® a try!

Visit us at
www.eHarlequin.com

The **2 FREE BOOKS** we send you will be selected from **SILHOUETTE ROMANCE®**, the series that brings you...a more traditional romance from first love to forever.

Books received may vary.

▼ DETACH AND MAIL CARD TODAY! ▼

*Scratch off the silver area to see what the Silhouette Reader Service has for you.*

*Silhouette®*
Where love comes alive™

# YES!
I have scratched off the silver area above. Please send me the **2 FREE** books and gift for which I qualify. I understand I am under no obligation to purchase any books, as explained on the back and on the opposite page.

315 SDL DH46                    215 SDL DH45

| | |
|---|---|
| FIRST NAME | LAST NAME |

ADDRESS

| | |
|---|---|
| APT.# | CITY |

| | |
|---|---|
| STATE/PROV. | ZIP/POSTAL CODE |

Offer limited to one per household and not valid to current Silhouette Romance® subscribers. All orders subject to approval.

©2001 HARLEQUIN ENTERPRISES LTD. ® and TM are trademarks owned by Harlequin Enterprises Ltd.

(S-R-04/02)

# THE SILHOUETTE READER SERVICE®—Here's how it works:

Accepting your 2 free books and gift places you under no obligation to buy anything. You may keep the books and gift and return the shipping statement marked "cancel." If you do not cancel, about a month later we'll send you 6 additional books and bill you just $3.15 each in the U.S., or $3.50 each in Canada, plus 25¢ shipping & handling per book and applicable taxes if any.* That's the complete price and — compared to cover prices of $3.99 each in the U.S. and $4.50 each in Canada — it's quite a bargain! You may cancel at any time, but if you choose to continue, every month we'll send you 6 more books, which you may either purchase at the discount price or return to us and cancel your subscription.

*Terms and prices subject to change without notice. Sales tax applicable in N.Y. Canadian residents will be charged applicable provincial taxes and GST.

If offer card is missing write to: Silhouette Reader Service, 3010 Walden Ave., P.O. Box 1867, Buffalo NY 14240-1867

DETACH AND MAIL CARD TODAY!

## BUSINESS REPLY MAIL
FIRST-CLASS MAIL    PERMIT NO. 717-003    BUFFALO, NY

POSTAGE WILL BE PAID BY ADDRESSEE

SILHOUETTE READER SERVICE
3010 WALDEN AVE
PO BOX 1867
BUFFALO NY 14240-9952

NO POSTAGE
NECESSARY
IF MAILED
IN THE
UNITED STATES

"Why?"

"I don't want to marry again."

"Why not?" He watched her uneasiness grow. "Or is it only the prospect of being married to me that's so unappealing?"

She lifted her chin. "It's difficult enough to make a marriage work when you're in love or think you're in love. We'd be going into this for all the wrong reasons."

"Bull. We'd be doing it for our children. Can you give me a better reason?" He took her elbow and urged her toward the couch where they both sat. "And we wouldn't be going into it with any ridiculous expectations, no stars in our eyes or dreams that won't come true."

"How exciting for us. You make marriage sound about as appealing as scrubbing the toilets."

"Look, I care about you. I don't want you hurt by rumors."

"I suspect there will be talk. Still, that's not a reason to marry."

"Are you still angry with me over your job?" he asked, taking her hand in his.

"Partly, but ever since you walked into that conference room, you've taken control of my life, like my ex—" She gave him an apologetic look. "Sorry. Guess I am making comparisons. I really don't mean to." She drew a deep breath before continuing. "I made myself a promise that I would never let anyone else run my life. But that's what you've done, what you're still doing."

He ran the pad of his thumb over her knuckles. "How?"

"You've moved me in here with you," she said, pulling her hand from his. "You were partly to blame for me losing my job, and now you want to get married. I'm sorry, Hunter, but I just can't do it. You're going way too fast for me."

"What if I slow things down, let you be in control?"

She laughed. After seeing he didn't share her humor, she continued. "You can't stop being yourself. It's your nature. I'm not saying being aggressive is bad necessarily. It's just not something I want. Your need to gain the upper hand will only get worse if we marry. Marrying for the sake of the children is something I'm not ready to consider."

She kept throwing out answers he didn't like, but he was at a loss of how to counter. He wondered if her sudden reluctance was a result of having heard about the trouble he'd gotten into as a teen. "Will you ever trust my judgment?"

Ashley gave him a doubtful look. "Probably not."

He released a long breath. "I really think this is what's best for us. What can I do to change your mind?"

"I don't know."

Her nearness made him long to touch her, hold her. He leaned closer until her breath fanned his lips, teasing him, inviting him to taste her once more despite the barrier created by her words. A barrier he intended to level, one kiss at a time. "It's not in my nature to give up without a fight."

"I know, but I don't want to fight." Her eyes softened. She angled toward him, her gaze dropping to his lips as if asking him to kiss her, inviting him to take what she offered.

And he wanted to take her up on that offer, couldn't remember when he'd last wanted anything so desperately. Something inside him wanted to take it to the limit, however far that might be, see how responsive she really might be. Only the next time he kissed her, Hunter feared there wouldn't be any holding back. Not like before.

"Fighting isn't what I had in mind." He glanced once more at her mouth and remembered the softness of her lips under his. He wanted to kiss her again. In fact, the closer he got, the more she leaned toward him, boneless…as if waiting for the touch of his mouth against hers. And maybe more. It would be so easy. He could lay her down right here, see how pliant she would be in his arms, see how far he could go. And, damn, that's exactly what he was primed and ready—hell, more than ready—to do. But at what cost? He didn't need to do that, couldn't do that, not even if Ashley was willing. As much as he would like to see where things might lead, Ashley was still under a doctor's care. And he had brought her here to take care of her, not to seduce her.

"If not fighting, Hunter, then what exactly did you have in mind?" she asked.

"I'm not sure." He brushed his thumb across the curve of her jaw and ached with need. He released her chin and shifted on the couch to ease his discomfort. Time. He needed time to think of how, other than seduction, to make Ashley change her mind about marrying him. Under different circumstances, he would bombard her with surprises, keep her off-guard, keep her guessing while applying subtle pressure. Like he did his opponents. But she wasn't an adversary, and he refused to treat her as such. He couldn't. He wouldn't. "You're making this tough on me."

"Tough?" she whispered. "In what way?"

"Bulldozing a matter to a resolution has always been my style. Walking away has never been an acceptable option." Until now because of her.

Ashley frowned. "That's what frightens me most."

And that's why, unlike other times when he'd instinctively made decisions for Ashley, wanting to shield and shelter her, he couldn't this time. He had to wait until she came around on her own without any pressure from him. But he had never been long on patience. He'd already made up his mind to marry her. Soon. "Do you think I would go behind your back and try to coerce or trick you into marrying me?''

"No, I don't think you would."

He hadn't been this surprised since learning his sperm had been used to impregnate a stranger. Recovering from the shock, he acknowledged her admission pleased him. "Whatever happens between us will be because we both want it."

He had to find a way to convince her marriage was the best solution. He wanted to protect Ashley from bastards like her boss. But more than wanting to keep her safe, he longed to kiss her, hold her, turn to her during the night. And as much as he tried not to think about it, he imagined how she would feel surrounding him.

She met his gaze. "You know, I never believed I would say this, but for some reason I feel you really mean what you're saying."

*Hell.*

Hunter shifted once more and leaned back. "I don't want to control you." He placed his hand over the swell of her abdomen. Seeing evidence of his children's growth sent warmth through him. "I only want to take care of you and my babies, make you happy. I want to do the right thing."

"But—"

"Just think about it." He stood. "If you need me, I'll be in the basement."

He felt her gaze on his back as he headed for the kitchen.

"You go down there every night, Hunter. What is it exactly that you do in the basement?"

"Nothing important." Physical labor to give him something to do with his hands. But mostly, it was where he went to keep from doing something stupid like holding and kissing Ashley again. If she kept looking at him with those liquid brown eyes that revealed far more than they concealed, he would do a hell of a lot more than just kiss her. And that was something he couldn't do until the doctor gave them the go-ahead, and Ashley wanted it, too. Unfortunately his mind had no control over the rest of his body. At least not where Ashley was concerned.

Hunter forced himself to put one foot in front of the other and refused to look back. He needed to think, to come up with a plan to keep his libido in check with Ashley living under the same roof. If he didn't know better, he would think she purposely taunted him by turning his bathroom into a panty hose and lace bra jungle. And the itty-bitty panties he'd found in his laundry had him analyzing just exactly how much skin that nonexistent scrap of material really covered. But more than that, he had become completely obsessed with wanting to run his hands over what it left exposed.

Hunter muttered under his breath as he opened the door to the basement and started down the stairs. He needed physical exertion—lots of it—to get his mind off Ashley. Fat chance. She had moved in and taken over his house and his head. And other parts of his body he tried his best to ignore.

He wanted to do things right so Ashley wouldn't pay the price for his foolishness years ago. So how did he go about convincing her marriage to a man who had a history of making mistakes was the best thing to do?

And if he did convince her to marry him, would he end up disappointing her, hurting her the same as he had his parents?

"Sit down, Hunter. I have something to say, and this time you're going to listen."

Hunter looked up from his desk to the dark figure in the

doorway, all smooth granite and polished marble. Immovable. Emotionless.

Buchanan Prescott Morgan.

His father.

Hunter settled his coffee cup on the desk and pushed to his feet. "I don't know what you want, but this is a bad time. I'm due in court in fifteen minutes."

"What in the hell do you think you're doing?"

He met his father's hard gaze, irritated that Buck could still make him feel guilty after all this time. And, for once, Hunter hadn't done anything wrong. "What are you talking about?"

Buck strode to the front of Hunter's desk and leaned forward, balancing his weight on his hands. "I'm going to give you some advice, Hunter. I hope this time you won't let your stubborn pride keep you from listening. The way I see it, if you really want to be the next D.A., then you can't act like you're still a kid who's not accountable for his actions."

Hunter circled his desk, a mixture of shock and anger ricocheting through him as he paced. "I don't know what you mean. I stand accountable for everything I do. Besides, nothing's official about Garrett leaving until he makes an announcement." Even though his boss had already told him he was moving back to his hometown, Hunter didn't feel obligated to share that news with Buck.

His father turned and leaned against the corner of Hunter's desk. "My sources are reliable. When Garrett leaves, you're next in line. Unless you mess up or are challenged, you'll automatically become district attorney."

Hunter knew exactly what his dad was getting at now and he resented the hell out of it. "What do you mean by messing up?"

"Rumor has it this woman you've got living with you is pregnant...and that she's claiming the baby is yours."

"It's not what you think."

His dad held up a hand to silence Hunter, same as he always had. "It never is." Buck stared at the toes of his shoes and rubbed the back of his neck. "I had hoped you'd learned your lesson years ago, but I can see you haven't. About this woman—"

"Leave Ashley out of it."

"I can't and you know it. Everything you do from here on out affects your career. Politics is a funny business. A community thinks a candidate should have morals. You were damned lucky last election that this town wanted Garrett as badly as they did. Otherwise, you would never have had a chance at getting this job. You've done a good job though, made a decent start toward making this town forget all the foolish things you did years ago. That doesn't mean they'll overlook you living and having a baby with an unmarried woman. Dammit, Hunter, if you want to be D.A., then you've got to change your ways."

"I have changed. That's what I'm trying to prove, but nobody can see beyond my past."

"They will if you'll let them, and that's why you've got to decide what you want. Can't you see, it's like you're rubbing their noses in the past. Once the papers get wind of Garrett's leaving, they'll dig up every bit of dirt they can find on you. They will pick your bones clean. God knows, with your history, they would have a feast. They'll also probe into your family."

It hurt that his father hadn't come out of concern for Hunter's future, but to safeguard his own reputation. "I can't help that. Ashley stays with me."

"How do you know her? Where does she come from?"

"Why? Are you concerned she's not good enough for me?"

"No, that's not it."

"Well, don't worry. She's better than I deserve, and I won't ask her to leave. I'll take my chances with the press." For once, Hunter wished he could sit down and explain everything to his father. But Buck had never listened, and Hunter had never wanted his father's advice. Not that he did now. It was a foolish thought, and he couldn't imagine why he'd had it. "How did you hear about Ashley?"

"That's not important." Buck let out a long breath. "If this woman matters so much that you're willing to risk everything, maybe you should consider marriage. You might be surprised at how much you'll like it. A wife would lend you a respectable, settled appearance and might get you elected."

Same song. Second verse. So typical of Buck, the politician. "For the record, I would never marry for the sake of appearances. Yeah, I want to be the next D.A., but not because it will make me fit in socially or make people accept me. I want it for the good I can do the community."

"Good campaign slogan if you can pull it off. Now, what about Ashley? Is she a good woman?"

Hunter didn't need time to consider the question "She's the best."

"Then, as the father of her baby, don't you think you owe it to her to do the right thing?"

As usual, his father hadn't heard a thing he'd said. Nothing new there. Hunter grabbed his briefcase and faced Buck. "I've already asked Ashley to marry me, but my proposal had nothing to do with getting elected."

"I'm pleased to hear that. I hope you're serious about straightening up this time. If not for yourself, then for her."

"She's the only reason I'm doing it. Now, if you'll excuse me, I'm due in court."

When Hunter tried to leave, Buck barred his way. "Do you plan to let your mother meet her?"

"I don't know if Ashley is ready for that just yet. Maybe later, when the time is right." Hunter wasn't sure the time would ever be right. Ashley had already asked about his family and he knew that sooner or later he would have to take her to dinner at his parents. Even though it seemed his father wasn't all that interested in meeting her, Hunter knew Ashley would charm Buck, same as she had him.

"The time is right now. Your mother is worried about you."

Hunter watched his father leave, noticing Buck had managed to have the last word, but then he always had. He thought about their conversation and his dad's comments about Ashley and marriage. He intended for things to work with Ashley, which is precisely why he had neglected to mention she had declined his proposal. Now he had to find a way to get her to say yes.

As much as it irritated Hunter to admit it, Buck was right in one respect. The town hadn't forgotten what he had done, and people gossiped. It was only a matter of time before someone said something to Ashley. Once she learned about the stunts he'd pulled as a troubled teen, Hunter feared she might leave, deciding he wasn't suitable.

It didn't matter that she might be correct. Nothing mattered anymore, except proving he would be a good husband and father. Somehow he had to convince Ashley to marry him.

## Chapter Seven

After a couple of weeks of twiddling her thumbs and spending her evenings alone, Ashley decided to take action. She glanced at the basement door as she placed her empty glass on the kitchen counter. The roar of a power tool came from below, the pitch higher, more of a whine than the sounds she'd heard earlier.

The noise beckoned her. She walked to the basement door, remembering Hunter's warning not to venture there, and placed her hand on the wood. The force of the offending screech from downstairs vibrated against her palm. The tingling glided up her arm and curled into the pit of her stomach, making her feel anxious and uneasy, the same way she felt whenever Hunter watched her. She shouldn't think about him in that way, or any way for that matter, but found herself missing him more with each tick of the clock.

After several weeks of persistent proposals, it now seemed as if Hunter had given up. With him being gone to work all day, she frankly resented his withdrawal at night and wished he would come upstairs. She didn't know when she'd come to the conclusion he'd avoided her but she couldn't shake the feeling any more than she could stop the need building inside her to be with him.

Ashley stepped away from the door. She walked to the window above the kitchen sink and studied the new green grass pushing its way through the thawed ground. Should she seek Hunter out or wait for him to surface?

She wet a washcloth and wiped the counter for the tenth time since Hunter had sought the seclusion of the basement. She didn't understand why his leaving her alone bothered her so much. Considering the many nights she had waited for her ex-husband to come home, she should be used to a solitary life. Only for some reason this wasn't at all the same.

Her ex had spent his evenings with loose women. At least Hunter stayed home…with his power tools. Between tramps and power tools, she believed Hunter had gotten the better deal.

She had allowed her ex to keep secrets for most of their six-year marriage. That was one mistake she wouldn't repeat. Another was letting any man tell her what to do. It was time to invade ''no man's land.'' Ashley gave the counter a determined swipe before tossing the rag into the sink. She crossed the room and tugged the door open, then winced at the piercing wail that blasted her. She covered her ears and carefully picked her way down the rickety staircase one step at a time. The absence of a handrail made her nervous, and she hugged the wall as she peered down into what appeared to be fog.

The pungent scent of freshly cut wood enveloped Ashley as she carefully descended into the cold dampness until her feet came to rest on the concrete floor. Bent over a table of sorts with his back to her, Hunter stood beneath a lone bulb that gave off a dull glow in the center of the room. Sawdust spewed in every direction. Fine particles tickled Ashley's nose, and she cupped her hand across her lower face.

She watched him for a long while, his thick muscles flexing and bunching beneath the tank top as he worked. The view of his backside—the tanned skin between the hem of his top and waistband of his faded jeans—made her mouth go dry. Or, perhaps it was the sawdust she inhaled. Or the way the baseball cap he wore backward looked so natural on him.

She could only guess how long she'd been standing there gaping when Hunter glanced over his shoulder as if sensing her presence. He did a double take before flipping off the machine and turning to face her. A sudden quiet filled the damp room as he removed a pair of safety glasses. His gaze fastened on her as he stood among floating particles of wood dust that glistened white and gold in the light of the overhead bulb.

He pitched the glasses on the table before he started toward her, his brow drawn into a frown. "Is something wrong?"

"No," she whispered, her gaze drifting to the width of his shoulders. "I'm fine." She wasn't fine at all though. Sawdust and tiny wood chips clung to the dark mat of hair visible at the neck of his tank top and down his muscled arms. Funny how a moment earlier she'd thought the basement musty and cold, but now seeing Hunter like this made it hot, incredibly hot.

"You shouldn't be here," he said, trying to herd her toward the stairs. "It's not safe. Let me help you upstairs."

He was right. It wasn't safe, but the danger came from Hunter, not the rickety steps. "Could we talk?"

"Talk?"

"Yes," she said, resisting the urge to glide her fingers across the contours of his face, to brush the sawdust from the arch of his brow and the chiseled plane of his cheek.

He shifted his weight to one hip. The jeans, worn white and frayed in places, molded to the sinew and muscle, making it clear Hunter Morgan did a lot more than just sit behind a desk.

Her gaze followed the denim down his long legs to the running shoes he sported without socks. He wore the casual attire with the same confidence as a pinstriped suit and designer shoes, his manner making it clear he dressed for himself without regard to the opinion of others.

Ashley thought him to be the most incredibly sensual man she'd ever known.

"What do you want to talk about?" he asked.

Talk? How could she carry on an intelligent conversation when she couldn't think of anything but him when he was near? And if she looked at him much longer with sweat glistening on his tanned upper body, Ashley knew she'd have to touch him. She forced her attention to the wooden spindle mounted on a machine. "Is that what caused so much noise?"

As she drew closer to the table, she saw three spindles, each one a mirror image of the others. Beside them rested what looked like a small rectangular feed trough. "What's all this?"

She sensed Hunter behind her, felt his warmth. "It's not done yet." He ran his hand over the spindle still connected to the machine, his touch gentle, almost reverent, as he smiled.

Ashley examined each piece, allowing her fingers to glide over the smooth surfaces, then turned to Hunter. "Are you making a cradle?"

"Yeah." He looked away and busied himself, running a

clean rag over one of the spindles, as if embarrassed by her discovery.

Another side of Hunter she hadn't known existed. "I had no idea you did this sort of thing. I suppose I should have, but renovating a house is different from making a cradle. You've done a beautiful job. I've never seen anything so exquisite."

"As soon as I'm through with this cradle, I'll start a second."

Her throat constricted with emotion. Seeing Hunter dusted with wood shavings, looking so casual, almost vulnerable, stole her breath just as his thoughtful unselfishness melted her heart. "One day our children will appreciate all your hard work."

He looked at her then, his eyes wistful. "This is the easy part. The tough stuff comes later. I see a lot of kids herded through the system. They're lost and crying out for help. They come from dysfunctional families. I won't let that happen to my children. That's why I'm determined to do right by them, why I want to be a part of their lives. I want to make a difference."

Ashley cleared the emotion from her throat. "I won't try to keep you from the babies. I know how much it means to you."

"But you won't marry me."

Did she dare lay it all on the line? Could she afford to do that? She had married once for love, and it had ended in heartbreak. If she refused to take a leap of faith, refused to allow Hunter completely into her life, would she be doing it to protect the children? Or out of her own fear?

She and Hunter might never share the special love her parents had, the happily-ever-after kind of love she longed for, but she knew he would always love and protect his children. Him making the cradles was a prime example of that. "No matter what I decide to do, I want to thank you for caring for our children and making these beautiful beds." But as she leaned forward on tiptoe to hug Hunter, Ashley admitted that him loving their children wouldn't be enough. She wanted more. She wanted a husband who loved her. But she'd already had her chance at love and failed. Now, she had to think of her children.

Hunter grasped her arms and stepped back. "I'm covered in sawdust. You'll get dirty."

She slid closer and wrapped her arms around his neck. "I don't care. You've done so much for me and the babies." She laid her head against him, his strong heart beating in her ear. "I don't know how I can ever thank you for everything."

"Ashley, I don't want your thanks. I want you to marry me."

She raised her head. "I'll work with you to raise our children, but to even consider marriage, there has to be more."

"More?" His gaze burned her with its intensity. "Don't tell me you haven't noticed this chemistry between us. I know you've felt it, too. It's undeniable. You may not have wanted to acknowledge it, but it's there."

She'd have to be dead not to notice, but she had no intention of admitting that to him. Still, lust wasn't the same thing as love. And if she couldn't have love, she didn't want anything. "I don't know what you mean."

"I think you do know. We've both known since we shared that kiss, but let me refresh your memory." Hunter's hands spanned her waist as he bent forward. His mouth touched hers, and his tongue traced the seam of her lips. Unable to deny her own need and the connection of which he had spoken, she opened to him. He took immediate advantage and slipped inside her mouth as he pulled her closer, tugging her nearer, until her breasts were crushed against the hard wall of his chest.

His hands stroked her back, making her breathless. Every sweep of his tongue was a dance of seduction that sent her senses reeling and her temperature soaring. She tilted her head to give him better access.

His hands skimmed the sides of her breasts before he broke the kiss, his breathing as ragged as her own. "Marry me."

"But—"

He pressed his finger across her lips. "I want to give our children every opportunity for a happy life. I want to do right by them and you. I want to make this thing between us work."

Hunter was willing to make a sacrifice by offering himself up on a marital platter in exchange for the right to be with and take care of his children. "We don't have to get married for you to see your children. I've already told you I won't keep you from seeing them."

"Is that why you think I proposed?"

"Isn't it?"

"No. Look, if you don't want to marry me, I understand, but I wish you'd at least be honest about it."

"Are you being honest?" she asked, still unsure of his true motives.

"Yes. I won't have my children growing up thinking they were another of my mistakes."

"Mistakes?" she asked, wondering what he meant.

"You know, Ashley, no one's perfect, and I'm no exception," he said, letting out a slow breath. "Forty percent of the teens I prosecute come from one-parent families. I'm ready and willing to do whatever it takes to keep my children from ending up there, but I can't do it alone."

She realized then Hunter had the children's best interests

at heart. He was putting into action what she had professed to do, always placing her children's needs ahead of all others. But could she do what he asked? "I don't know."

"I want my children to have a good home," he continued. "*If* you'll marry me, we can do this together."

She thought about that a moment. "Do you mean a marriage in name only?"

He studied her. "Is that what you want?"

She licked her lips and tasted him. "I don't know if I can go to your bed knowing there's nothing else between us."

"We have our children and this attraction. A lot of people marry with less than that. Still, I respect your candor. I don't want to pressure you into making a decision. What if we let it ride, let nature take its course?"

She just knew he was up to something, but what? "What do you mean?"

"I think we ought to marry and leave everything else as it is now. If the time comes when we're both ready for things to change between us," he said, his gaze capturing and holding hers, "then all the better that it does. I believe everything will work out if we let it."

Ashley knew in that moment that Hunter intended to do his utmost to persuade her. And if the kiss they'd just shared was any indication, chances of her refusing him were slim to none. "I don't know—"

"Look, Ashley. If you'll marry me, then I promise not to put any pressure on you. We'll just take it one day at a time."

She wondered if he could hear her heart pounding. "Would we continue with separate bedrooms or share a room, a bed?"

"I won't lie. I want you in my bed, but where you sleep is up to you." He gave her one of his bone-melting looks that made her admit that in his bed, in his arms, is where she wanted to be, not that she intended to tell him. "You know, sometimes things happen that we don't necessarily plan. Let's not worry about it, just go with the flow and see where it takes us."

How could she not worry when every minute she spent with Hunter made her fall a little more under his spell? She had to keep her eyes wide open, make decisions based on what she knew to be true. Problem was, she couldn't think of anything, except his admission that he wanted her in his bed. "I don't know, Hunter. I need time to think."

"Time is a luxury we don't have." He splayed his fingers over her stomach. "Your pregnancy is already showing."

Her breath caught as his hand moved slowly over her stomach. "I know."

His gaze lingered on her, assessed her as did his palm on her tummy. "Ashley, have you said anything to anyone about staying here?"

"Only the personnel department so they could send me my last paycheck, but other than that and giving Dr. Rollins my new mailing address, no. Why?"

He shrugged and turned his attention to a spindle. "Just wondering."

Ashley watched, unable to look away, as he ran his fingers over the wood.

"You know, it sounds crazy, but I always dreamed of making furniture for my children one day, sturdy items they could keep for their own babies. But I never got the opportunity before."

Ashley caught a glimpse of what looked like pain skittering across his features. "What do you mean *before?*"

"It was a long time ago."

"Hunter, will you tell me?"

He raked his fingers through his hair. "There was a child."

Her heart skipped a beat. "You have another child?"

"No. It— There is no child now. I never had the chance to do anything like this. That's why it's so important to me. Please don't push me away. Don't put me through that again."

Ashley felt his pain as if it were her own and wondered how she could possibly turn him down now. Still, did she dare believe Hunter's promise? She had trusted a man once and he'd broken her heart. Her only reason for considering Hunter's proposal now was to give her children a father who would love them without reservation. More than needing to learn what had happened in Hunter's past to leave him scarred and hurting, she suddenly wanted to ease his pain. She wanted to give him the one special gift the other woman—whoever she was—hadn't been able to. It would be a huge risk, marrying Hunter, but that risk could just possibly lead to a lifetime. A lifetime father for their babies, not just a weekend daddy. As scared as she was of making another mistake, this time it wasn't just about her. It was about their children…and Hunter, a man who was willing to give up his freedom for their children.

Could she do this? Could she marry Hunter, knowing she would be risking another heartache? Because God help her, she was falling for this man. And that scared her worst of all.

"I'll marry you."

"By the power vested in me by the state of Texas, I now pronounce you husband and wife. You may kiss the bride."

Hunter turned in the judge's chambers to face Ashley, the woman he had just sworn to love and protect, and noted her lack of color. Was she suffering from morning sickness? Or did she already regret having married him? Then again, maybe her thoughts centered on the wedding night that wouldn't be. Exactly where his thoughts were now.

He wanted to calm her fears, tell her he had no intention of sequestering her in a jury room to exercise his husbandly rights following the ceremony. But damned if that wasn't exactly what he found himself wanting to do…just as soon as he sealed their vows with a kiss.

Hunter hooked his forefinger beneath her chin and brushed his lips over hers in a chaste kiss. He longed to circle her waist with his hands, pull her against him and deepen the kiss. But he didn't.

She was anything but fine. Now wasn't the time for another kiss even if it was the only act of consummation they would share for now.

She opened her eyes and attempted a smile that wobbled before disappearing.

Judge McLennan stepped forward. "Let me be the first to offer my congratulations." He shook Hunter's hand and then kissed Ashley's cheek. "If you'll excuse me, several attorneys are pacing in the hallway. I imagine they're wanting to see me."

As the judge left his office, Jared, whom she had met ten minutes earlier along with his wife, moved between Hunter and Ashley to kiss her cheek and hug her. "I don't know what you did to get Hunter to the altar, but it's time someone made an honest man of him. Welcome to the family."

Lauren stepped forward to hug Hunter and then Ashley and to offer her congratulations. "So, where are you honeymooning?"

Hunter cursed himself for not offering an appropriate honeymoon. Well, that wasn't technically true. He had thought of it, but only in the sense that even if they slept together, it wouldn't be a real wedding night. Not without making love. He couldn't help but wonder if that was the pattern of their future together. Like hell. Not if he had anything to say about it. "I have to be in court on Monday, so we thought we might go to a little bed-and-breakfast or some out-of-the-way place so we can have the weekend to ourselves."

Ashley's gaze swung to Hunter, reflecting her surprise at his words. Her eyes had widened, but she remained silent when he caught and squeezed her hand in assurance.

Lauren's expression turned wistful and she sighed. "Could we treat you to a celebration dinner before you take off?"

If Ashley's color was any indication, Hunter needed to get her out of here now. "How about a rain check?" He slipped his arm around Ashley's waist and held her close to his side. "Since the weekend is all the honeymoon we'll have for a while, we're anxious to get started."

Jared gave Hunter a probing look. "When you get back in town, we'll have you and the rest of the family over to dinner."

Hunter met his brother's gaze. "Yeah. That would be great."

His brother nodded and the tension in Hunter's neck and shoulders eased somewhat.

"Hunter Morgan, you old son of a gun, is it true you just got shackled?"

Dropping his hold on Ashley, Hunter turned and shook hands with Dan Phillips, another local lawyer. "Yes, and we're on our way out."

"Good political move. Stroke of genius. Great strategy." The attorney winked at Ashley. "Is this the little lady?"

Hunter could see the wheels turning in Ashley's mind. From the look on her face, she hadn't missed Phillips's pointed comment. A keen intellect was hidden behind her demure facade, just like he knew a great body was concealed beneath the cream-colored suit. He had to get her out of here before she heard the rumors that the district attorney was leaving. He wanted to be the one to tell her, but not now. There would be plenty of time for that later. Besides, he didn't want her jumping to the wrong conclusion about the upcoming election and why he had rushed her to the courthouse. "Ashley, this is—"

"Dan Phillips with the Sherwood firm." She shook the hand the attorney held out. At his questioning look, she continued, "I work for Richard Williams at Barnett & Williams."

"Worked. Past tense," Hunter interjected.

The attorney raised a brow. "I thought you looked familiar."

Hunter took her elbow. "If you'll excuse us, we need to be on our way."

With that, Hunter turned his back on the lawyer and rushed Ashley through hurried goodbyes to Jared and Lauren. Then he steered her from the room.

"What was all that about good political moves and strategies?" she asked as he held open the door leading outside.

*A lawyer with a big mouth.* "Who knows? I've never known Phillips to make much sense."

"I get the feeling he's another lawyer you don't much like."

Hunter placed his hand at her spine as they crossed the street. "I think his license should have been pulled a long time ago." He glanced at her then as her hair glistened in the early afternoon sun. "Enough about lawyers. I should have told you before now how nice you look."

"Thanks. I won't be wearing this outfit again anytime soon. It's cutting off my oxygen. I can't wait to get it off."

Desire kicked Hunter low in the gut, swift and intense,

at the thought of helping her undress. He fought it, reminding himself there wouldn't be a wedding night. At least not for a while. "Let's go home and pack."

She studied him with cautious eyes. "Why?"

Because he didn't feel married, not like he'd expected. But more than that, he wanted to give Ashley a wedding night so she'd feel married…to him. "People generally spend their honeymoon alone."

"And we wouldn't be alone at your place?" she asked. Her voice had a breathless quality that captivated him.

The pearl necklace she wore drew his gaze to the hollow at the base of her throat where her pulse throbbed. "There's always the threat that someone might call or drop by."

"How would that be a problem?"

He couldn't stop his smile. "It's our honeymoon. I'm supposed to keep you in bed until Sunday night."

A look of panic crossed her face. "But, Hunter—"

"Look, I haven't forgotten my promise. You've had a tough couple of weeks, and I want you to get some rest. That's all." *Liar.* That wasn't at all what he'd meant, but she had looked ready to bolt and he didn't want to cause her any more anxiety.

Hunter supposed he could get them adjoining rooms or maybe twin beds to put her mind at ease. Like hell he would. Not on their honeymoon. He cursed himself for promising to not pressure her, not that it mattered since she was still under a doctor's care. Still, he wanted them sleeping together soon. Why not start tonight? After all, it was their honeymoon. And he wanted to hold her.

Now all he had to do was figure out how he was supposed to share a bed with Ashley and keep his promise.

*Married.*

Ashley stretched, still feeling lethargic from her nap, and

glanced around the room Hunter had been lucky enough to get when they'd arrived at the bed-and-breakfast that afternoon.

She smiled at the memory of how he'd swept her off her feet and lowered her onto the bed they would share as man and wife, his weight pressing her deeper into the mattress. The way his eyes had darkened as he'd braced his arms on either side of her head made her feel like a nervous bride, attractive, and maybe even a little bit desirable. But then after a too brief brush of his lips across hers, he'd pushed off the bed, muttering a succinct curse about stupid promises followed by a terse apology, and the door had slammed shut behind him.

She rolled to stare at the other side of the bed, the plumped pillow and the undisturbed patchwork quilt. This was their honeymoon, the first day of their new life together. She didn't know where Hunter had gone. Or when he would be back.

The plain gold band on her left hand drew her attention. She couldn't believe she had done the one thing she'd sworn never to do again—marry. And she'd married another lawyer. To make matters worse, she'd found herself noticing things about him, things she shouldn't care about, things that pointed to the fact that she was falling hard for him. Obviously pregnancy had affected her mind. What other reason could there be for placing herself in a position to be hurt all over again. Nothing had changed, including her name, except for the "e" in Morgen becoming an "a."

At her first wedding there had been flowers, satin and lace in abundance. At the extravagant reception, the champagne had flowed. If that marriage had failed after such a majestic start, what possible hope did she have with Hunter?

This morning's ceremony had been nothing more than

an exchange of reluctant pledges given in a judge's somber chambers. Despite the doubt that choked her, she had somehow managed to recite the standard vows. Still, making promises she didn't know if she could keep seemed all wrong. Maybe that's why the words had carried such a false ring. She couldn't help but feel that today—the functional wedding and now this phony honeymoon—was an omen of her life with Hunter. It broke her heart, because after that night in his basement, she had dared to hope they might one day share more than just a name. If Hunter's absence was any indication, she had obviously been wrong.

He had been right to insist they marry for the sake of their children. Only now she realized that wouldn't be enough.

The bedroom door opened and Hunter peeked in. "Good, you're awake. Are you hungry?"

Ashley threw back the covers and pushed herself into a sitting position. She tried to convince herself she wasn't glad to see him, but knew she'd failed when he came inside and sat beside her on the edge of the bed.

"You heard my stomach growling, didn't you?" she asked. Or maybe he'd heard the beat of her heart as she stared at the T-shirt stretched tight across his shoulders that seemed to fill the room.

He smiled that crooked smile she had become so fond of and, as always, her heart did a little stutter-step before she reminded herself of the reason they had married.

"We missed dinner downstairs," he said, "so I thought if you felt up to it we might go out."

"I'd like that. I didn't realize I'd slept so long. You should have gotten me up."

"You needed to rest," he said as he leaned forward and cupped her cheek. "You don't look so tired now. What are you in the mood for?"

She knew he meant food, but if he got an inch closer she would be tempted to lie back on the bed and see if he followed. He had earlier that day. Maybe he would again. Did she really want him to or was she experiencing emotional overload because of the wedding? Yeah, she finally admitted to herself. She wanted *him*. The thought of kissing him sounded about as good as anything she could think of. In fact, at the moment she couldn't think of much else.

"Ashley?"

Realizing he waited on her answer, she shrugged. "I, uh, I'm easy."

One corner of his mouth twitched before lifting in a wide grin. "Is that right? Well, I'll tuck that bit of information away for later." He winked at her, then cleared his throat. "Now about dinner, do you like Italian?"

She enjoyed their easy banter even though her face burned. "I love Italian." If he kept looking at her like he was now, she would have to be careful. Otherwise, she would certainly fall completely for him, and that wouldn't be smart. So long as things didn't go beyond a few stolen kisses, Ashley believed she would be able to keep things in perspective. She might have married Hunter for the sake of the children, but she wasn't willing to risk her heart again.

He pushed to his feet and offered his hand. "Great. Let's go."

"I need to change," she said, accepting his hand as she indicated her loose T-shirt and stretch slacks.

He stepped back and allowed his gaze to slide over her, lingering in all the places it shouldn't, making her grow warm. "You're fine. The restaurant I have in mind is casual."

"All right. Let me drag a comb through my hair."

He moved closer and reached out to brush back an errant curl from her cheek. "I like it this way."

She ran her fingers through her hair, knowing without looking how bushy it was after her nap. "You can't be serious. It's a mess."

Hunter focused his attention on her hair before meeting her gaze. "No, it's the way every man wants his woman to look."

*His woman?* "What do you mean?"

"Like you just crawled out of bed."

"But I have."

"Like you've just been made love to, good and long and hard. Every man at the restaurant will think we've spent the whole afternoon having the best sex of our lives."

The way Hunter looked at her sent a rush of yearning through her. "Oh."

He smiled. "And they'll wish they could trade places with me."

Heat crawled up Ashley's neck and settled in her cheeks. She stepped around him and crossed the room to put some distance between them. It was difficult, if not impossible, to ignore the seductive statement and the promise in his blue eyes. If she didn't get them both out of this room, she might well be tempted to share his bed, consider what he'd just mentioned. But they hadn't married out of love, and it would be dangerous to let herself pretend they had. "I appreciate what you're trying to do, Hunter. But it isn't necessary."

"And just what do you think that would be?"

"Seduce me with words so I won't point out you got a room with only one bed."

"Guilty as charged."

Ashley was taken aback by his direct answer. "What

about your promise not to pressure me, that I could choose where I slept?''

"If it will make you feel better, I'll sleep on the couch."

"Oh." She tried to deny her disappointment.

"I want you in my bed, but I won't pressure you."

"We need to remember the real reason behind our marriage."

"The reason being our children?"

She turned back to face him. "Of course."

"We also agreed to make our marriage as close to real as possible so it would have a better chance of working."

Ashley suddenly felt very tired and wanted to lean into Hunter. Not allowing herself that weakness, she hugged her waist instead. "Yes, for the children, but you don't have to treat me like a normal wife. Meaning you don't have to lie about how you feel about me…us."

"I haven't lied. You are my wife and I intend to treat you as such. I don't know what the future holds. Neither of us do, but I don't think we should rule out certain possibilities. Let's just give it a chance and wait and see."

She knew what possibilities he meant. Could she let him make love to her, knowing he might never feel the way she did?

He sighed. "I'm going to be honest with you. You're a very beautiful, very desirable woman. If things were different, I wouldn't let you out of this room until five minutes before time to go home day after tomorrow."

His declaration had made her throat go dry as Texas grass in August. "I didn't, I mean I, uh, didn't realize."

He walked toward her, not stopping until she felt his heat. "That's just how I feel, but I'm not going to make you do anything you don't want. It's your decision."

Hunter had sounded confident that she would come to him. Deep down, she couldn't help but worry about the possibility herself. She'd never known a man more irresistible, especially wearing a tank top and wood shavings.

"We'll go whenever you're ready," he said.

*Whenever she was ready.* Ready for what? To go to the restaurant? That wouldn't take long, but Ashley didn't think she would ever be ready. Not for Hunter. Not for all the things he had just said, much less the way he made her feel. And most certainly not for the things he suddenly had her considering.

Ashley had always been a foolish romantic and had risked ever finding happily ever after by marrying Hunter, but it was a chance she had taken for her children. Now, she found herself wanting to explore the possibilities he had mentioned. She had always been cautious, done the right thing, but safe wasn't a word that came to mind when she thought of Hunter. And even though they couldn't do anything until after the doctor gave them the okay, she couldn't shake the thought of spending the night in the security of his arms. "Hunter."

"Yeah."

"You said where I slept was my choice."

"Yeah."

"I want to sleep in that bed…with you."

# Chapter Eight

Later that night, Hunter turned away from the bed, still plagued by thoughts of the night to come, of holding Ashley in his arms. His fingers paused on the buttons of his shirt as he saw her standing silhouetted in the bathroom doorway.

A cartoon character whose name eluded him decorated the front of her long red T-shirt that stopped just above her knees. Her sleeping attire wasn't anything special, not at all what he'd expected for their honeymoon, but this wasn't a typical wedding night. Nothing about their relationship—how they'd gotten together or the reasons behind their marriage—had been typical. And neither was the way his heart lurched at the sight of her.

"Hunter, did you not hear me? I asked why your parents didn't come to our wedding."

"I heard." He removed his shirt, stalling for time while he tried to figure out what he could do or say to keep from having to talk about his parents on his honeymoon. It was bad enough that he couldn't give Ashley the kind of wedding night she deserved. Dredging up the past would only worsen the tension already coiled tight in his gut. He made the mistake then of looking at her, really looking at her and suppressed a groan.

His mind understood he couldn't make love to Ashley, but remembering the promise he'd given didn't stop him from wanting her. He admitted it was a no-win situation and forced his thoughts back to the minute details of untying and removing his shoes. If he didn't find something to distract himself from the way the bathroom light outlined her body in vivid detail, he was going to have to sleep in his truck.

"Hunter, what's wrong?"

"Nothing." Everything. He didn't think he should mention that looking at her aroused him. Not that it wasn't obvious even after she flipped off the bathroom light and stepped toward him. If she knew the danger she was in, she would run back into the bathroom and lock the door. That would be the safe thing to do. The smart thing to do. Because at the moment, he had the self-control of a fifteen-year-old with an excess of testosterone.

She paused an arm's length away and looked up at him. "Hunter, are you all right?"

"Yeah." The hell he was. He was anything *but* all right and needed to think about something other than the way her T-shirt dipped and swayed with her movements, revealing her long shapely legs. He tugged hard on his belt with hands that shook and pulled it from the loops of his jeans while she watched his every movement and in the process drove him to the brink of insanity.

Instead of talking about himself and his family, he would rather bury his face in the curve of Ashley's neck and give in to her innocent charm. Maybe that wasn't such a good idea either. "My parents weren't there, because I didn't invite them."

Brows knit, she looked almost hurt as she settled on the bed and slid between the sheets. "Why not?"

"It's complicated." So was this arrangement. If Ashley had any idea of how good she looked with her auburn hair fanned across the pillow, how he longed to take her in his arms and make slow crazy love to her she would call 9-1-1. He thought better of it, because he didn't want to frighten her after she'd agreed to share the bed with him tonight. It wasn't what he'd hoped she'd say, but still, it was a start. Hunter moved to the opposite side of the bed and switched off the small table lamp, then he unbuttoned and unzipped his jeans and removed them, wondering if she still watched or had turned away.

"I'm not sure I understand. We're talking about your parents."

He stretched out on the bed and turned to face her, wanting to kiss her into silence. "Look, Ashley, you may have come from nurturing parents who cared about you, but not all families are like that. Suffice it to say not inviting them was best."

"Are you ashamed of me?"

His gut tightened at the little catch in her voice. He couldn't believe she'd thought such a thing, and fought the urge to pull her into his arms. "Of course not."

"Will you tell me about them?"

Hunter wasn't sure he could, wasn't sure he wanted to dredge up the past, but mostly he wasn't ready for her to learn about the man she had married. Eventually she would have to hear the truth, and one day he would tell her so they could move forward with their life. Still, he feared that once she knew, she would be as disgusted with him as he was with himself. And that she might decide she'd made a mistake by marrying him.

He couldn't tell her, didn't want to talk about it, not yet anyway. And there was only one way he knew to draw her away from her current train of thought. He remembered his promise not to pressure her, but if a kiss or two was what it took to keep from having to tell her about his past, then he would do it. Just to distract her, nothing more.

Hunter pulled her closer and nibbled on her bottom lip, doing his best to draw her attention to what he was doing. When she sighed, he pulled away. "My folks had their hands full with me. I was always doing stuff, getting into trouble."

"A lot of kids go through difficult times—"

He pressed his mouth to hers once more, snaking his arm around her waist, tugging her against him until they touched from chest to knee.

She tore her lips from his and drew back for air. "Hunter, we really can't do anything."

"I know we can't, not completely, but just let me touch you." He skimmed his fingertips down her back, pleased when she shivered. He would stop when the time came, but for now, he didn't want her thinking.

She touched his arm. "What sort of things did you do?"

"Do?" he asked, having his own difficulty concentrating on anything except the way Ashley's fingers sifted through the hair on his chest.

"To get into trouble?"

Shame coursed through him. He couldn't tell her about how he'd gotten caught egging cars, painting graffiti and busting out streetlights. Not now. Not when Ashley was finally starting to accept him. "I did pretty much anything that would get me attention."

"Attention. From whom?"

He caught her hand and nipped at her fingers so she could no longer drive him to distraction or use them as a barrier to keep them apart. "People," he said, as he moved her hand to his shoulders and blazed a trail of kisses down her throat.

Anxiety mixed with desire filled Hunter. It had as much to do with the events from his past as it did with the groan that escaped Ashley's mouth and the way her fingers caressed his nape.

"What people?" she asked in a husky voice as she snuggled against him, driving him closer to the ragged edge of his control.

"My parents," he said, brushing his mouth over hers until he no longer wanted to stop.

"Why?"

"Why what?" he asked, losing his train of thought when she nibbled his bottom lip. He ran his hand up her side to cup her breast. Her gasp almost undid him and he pulled away.

"I don't remember," she whispered.

Hunter never wanted to let her go. He knew he shouldn't, but he wanted her. With the same breath, he knew, too, he couldn't stop what she was doing to him. What she'd been doing to him ever since he'd met her.

His mouth settled with firm possession on hers. It felt so good, so right. So perfect.

He reminded himself of his promise and vowed to leave her as he had earlier in the day. But what little strength he had abandoned him or maybe it was that his need for her was so much greater than before. He would stop later before things went too far, but for now he needed to hold her. Just a little longer. Then he would go outside, walk off his need for her, and sleep in his truck. He wouldn't break his promise and there was no way he could share this bed with Ashley and not have her. Not now. Maybe not ever.

Just one more kiss and he would go. Her lips parted beneath his as his hands whisked over her curves until they came to rest on the rise of her belly where his children lay nestled.

*His children.* A bucket of ice water couldn't have been more effective. He pulled away. It took a moment before his ragged breathing allowed him to speak. "I'm sorry. I shouldn't have let things go so far."

She ran her hand down his arm, a simple touch that jolted him. The whisper of her breath across his skin aroused him, made him feel like he'd come home, as if in her arms was where he really belonged. "I understand."

If she only knew how tight he was strung, she wouldn't look at him with eyes that had grown dark with desire or touch him the way she was now. "I want you, Ashley, more than you can possibly know, but I won't break my word. And I won't do anything that might hurt the babies. We really can't make love, can we? I mean if you decided that's what you wanted, too?"

"No. I'm afraid not. I called Dr. Rollins yesterday. He said it might be okay, but he would prefer to check me again before we resumed relations."

"*Resumed* relations?"

"I didn't tell him we had never... He assumed..."

Hunter silenced her with an all too brief brush of his lips. "I understand. I'll behave myself." Being good was the very last thing he wanted at the moment, but only a real jerk would break his word and make love to Ashley after the problems she'd had. He'd almost blown it tonight and wouldn't make another mistake, not where she was concerned. Not when it would endanger his children.

In the past, he'd never been any good at doing the right

thing and most times welcomed whatever trouble he found. Now more than ever he had to control himself, and he would, even if it meant spending the rest of his life in a cold shower. When Ashley had exchanged vows with him today, she had given him her trust. No way would he let her down. He resigned himself to bear the frustration of the long night ahead alone.

He knew all about temptation and being alone, but this time was different. This time if he messed up, the price he would pay could well be the lives of his children. And the trust of a woman he didn't deserve.

Ashley lay beside Hunter, waiting for his breathing to change so she would know he slept. After a while, she tried to inch away from him, remembering how he had rocked her world with only a few kisses. Now she found herself facing him, inhaling the musky fragrance that was uniquely his own, his right leg, thrown over hers, holding her captive.

She couldn't remember when she had last been so content, yet so afraid. She wasn't really sure what had happened, except that Hunter had provided piecemeal answers to her questions and kissed her. Then, she had ceased to recall what he had said, only that the things he'd done with his mouth were unlike anything she had ever known. And when he had pulled away, she'd wanted nothing more than to follow him so he could kiss her again.

This time away with Hunter had been so different, and she wished they didn't have to go home on Sunday. Tonight, instead of rushing back to work as had been Hunter's habit of late, he had lingered over their dinner as if there was no reason to hurry, nowhere to go. He had smiled, been charming, intoxicating.

Hunter had proven by marrying her that he was willing

to make sacrifices for their children. Ashley had met him halfway by entering into a loveless marriage. She'd thought that if she could keep her emotions out of it, then she would be able to sleep with him and everything would be all right. Only nothing had prepared her for the overpowering need Hunter's kisses had awakened, or the way he had touched her tenderly, reverently, almost as if he really cared. Almost as if he loved her.

Being with him tonight had been special, even though they hadn't made love. Much more special than she was ready to admit. In part, she thought, because Hunter had been true to his word. He had kissed her, and when things had gotten somewhat out of hand, he had pulled away.

She had to admit Hunter was right. There was something between them, something as intangible as the emotional walls she'd erected to protect her heart from another beating. Walls that he had torn down with lingering kisses and slow caresses. She admitted she cared for him, probably more than she should. And, if what he said was true, he wanted things to work, but could he come to care for her? Is that really what she wanted?

In that moment she knew she wanted his love. Worse still, she knew that in spite of her attempt to hold herself apart from him, she was in very real danger of falling in love with him. She refused to let it happen. Not again.

She would wait until he fell asleep and then slip from the bed and go to the sofa. But in the quiet of the room as the silver light of the moon slipped through the curtains, Hunter whispered, "If I'd had any say in who would mother my children, I couldn't have made a better choice than you."

Ashley felt the hot rush of tears sting the back of her eyes when the emotional dam around her heart shattered.

She was more miserable than ever, because she had fallen in love with Hunter. The father of her children.

Ashley surveyed the nursery from her rocking chair. They had worked on it almost every night the past month, and now it was finished. She stopped the chair's movement as Hunter wound the music box hidden beneath the soft fur in the back of a stuffed teddy bear—his newest purchase for the babies.

*Hush little baby, don't say a word. Daddy's going to buy you a mockingbird.*

The lines at the corners of Hunter's eyes crinkled as he smiled at her off-key singing. "What do you think?" he asked.

She thought he was the most thoughtful husband and father in the whole world and could easily envision spending the rest of her life with him. "I hope you don't intend to continue this practice of bringing the babies gifts every Friday."

He looked wounded. "What's wrong with me getting a few things? I want them to know how special they are to me."

"They'll know." His actions made his feelings so obvious, especially now that he'd dropped his guard a little more.

Hunter sat cross-legged on the carpet, his gaze on the matching cradles he had carried from the basement the night before. "Do you think these look smaller than they did downstairs? I'm not sure I made them big enough."

"They'll be fine. Our babies will weigh less than normal because they're twins."

He opened the package of disposable diapers beside him and withdrew one. Unfolding it, he placed the bear in the center and tugged and affixed the tabs. When he lifted the stuffed animal, the diaper slipped off. "This is harder than it looks."

"No worse than going up against hardened criminals."

Hunter sent her a sexy grin that melted her heart. "Well, I've never had to diaper an accused felon."

Ashley laughed and joined him on the carpet. She removed the diaper, then placed it open on the floor. "Okay, put the bear's bottom in the center."

"Like this?"

"Perfect. Bring the front portion up. Then pull the back forward until it's snug and press the tab in place. Now you do the other side."

After Hunter had finished, he smiled, his features relaxed, making him look young and carefree as he leaned to brush his lips against hers. Two months ago she wouldn't have believed things could be this way between them.

The temptation to let him deepen the kiss grew strong, but she placed a hand on his chest. She hoped the doctor would give them the okay to make love at her next visit.

Hunter stood and put the diapers and bear away. "Is there anything else you wanted to do in here tonight?"

Ashley accepted the hand he offered and got up. She moved to the cribs and ran her hand along the spindles. "No. I guess not."

"Is something wrong?"

"No. I'm just anxious for the waiting to be over."

Hunter came up behind her and, wrapping both arms around her, splayed his hands on her stomach. "You're halfway there."

Ashley looked at Hunter over her shoulder. "Keeping track?"

He smiled. "Yeah. I got a book called *Daddy In Waiting*. It's pretty interesting."

She arched her back. "You'll have to tell me what it says."

"If you'll read the next chapter to me, I'll rub your back."

It sounded heavenly. "You've got a deal."

Actually, she's the one who had gotten a deal when she had married Hunter. She'd had some doubts in the beginning, but now things couldn't be better. This past month with Hunter had been wonderful. Once their babies were born, life would be perfect.

After getting very little sleep since his marriage, and not for the reason most people would think, Hunter was exhausted and wanted to go home and go to bed. Problem was, he wanted Ashley in that bed with him. Damn his promise to not push her. And damn him for wanting her so much. Having to keep his hands off her was wearing him down to the point where each night he lay in bed thinking about her in the next room, wondering why she hadn't come to his bed after they'd returned from their honeymoon. If he didn't get a good night's sleep soon, he would pass out on his feet. He checked his watch for the third time in three minutes and swore under his breath.

The door to his office opened and Garrett Tyler entered. "Do you have a minute?"

He wanted to ignore Garrett's summons and hurry home, but the frown on the D.A.'s brow changed Hunter's mind. "Is something wrong?"

"Nothing more than the usual hassles." Garrett closed the door before raking his sun-streaked hair back with both hands. "I've wanted to talk to you about the specifics of my plans for some time now, certainly before they became fodder for the gristmill, but things have been kind of complicated."

Hunter circled his desk and sat on one corner. "I understand."

Garrett paused in his pacing to study him. "We haven't had much time to discuss how you feel about taking over as D.A. If no one else throws their hat in the race, you're going to get it all dumped in your lap."

"I haven't given it much thought. I've had a lot on my mind lately."

Garrett looked out the window. "Your new bride?"

Hunter smiled. "Yeah, among other things." Two other things to be exact.

"I'm not sure there's anything I can say that you don't already know about what I do. Being district attorney is a great job, but it's demanding as all hell. It's not eight to five and the pay's not as much as you could make in private practice."

"The thought of going into private practice has never appealed to me. I'm not cut out for a sedate life probating last will and testaments and scrutinizing business contracts."

"This is a big decision, Hunter. Getting married makes you look at things differently. Just think about it and let me know." Garrett turned to face Hunter. "Time's running out. If this is what you want, the county has asked for my thumbs-up."

Tension coiled in Hunter's gut. "Do you have a problem with giving your approval?"

"Your work is falling behind. You can't afford for the voters to think you can't handle the load."

"Garrett, you know I've always put in a ridiculous amount of hours. That hasn't changed, but our workload has."

"There's no money in the county's budget for help. You're just going to have to put in more hours." Garrett paused to meet Hunter's gaze. "You don't have a choice. If you're serious about taking over when I leave, then the job has to come first, ahead of everything else in your life. Hell, it's got to be your life. I know you're trying to make the adjustment of having a wife and pretty soon kids, but if giving this job the time it requires is something you can't do, then maybe you ought to consider private practice or going in with your dad and brother."

Hunter pushed off the desk to block Garrett's path when he tried to go around him. "Has Buck talked to you?"

Garrett shrugged. "Yeah. He came to express some concern over your recent court performance."

"What did he say?"

"He's not sure you're mature enough to handle the responsibility of this job. He asked my opinion."

Damn his father. Would he ever accept that Hunter didn't want or need his interference? "And your answer was?"

"I personally think you could handle it."

The tension in Hunter's shoulders eased. "Thanks for the vote of confidence."

Garrett moved once more to stare outside, his arms braced on either side of the window. "I'm going to tell you something strictly off the record because I don't want you going into this blind. If I recommend you for this position, I won't be doing you any favors. This job will eat you alive. The combination of the long hours, the nature and stress of the work and constantly being under public scrutiny will take its toll. I'll be frank with you. This job has kicked my butt. I'm burned out. I just can't do it anymore."

"Is that Meyers case still bothering you?"

"That's part of it."

"Garrett, we both know that kind of thing happens. Deadbeats get off on technicalities all the time. It's not your fault the guy walked."

"Maybe. Maybe not." Garrett exhaled a slow breath. "I feel like everything in my life is spiraling out of control. I'm going back home to Forestburg, Texas, in the hill country. I need to find some peace."

"A while back I suspected there was a woman. Is that it?"

Garrett regarded Hunter over one shoulder. "At one time there might have been, but... No, there's no one."

Despite his boss's denial, Hunter still believed a woman was involved, but he would respect Garrett's refusal to discuss it. It was amazing how women sometimes complicated all the issues.

Garrett pushed away from the window, then crossed to a chair and sank into it. Deep grooves etched the corners of his mouth, a measure of the man's misery. "About this job, make sure it's what you want, because the price you'll pay will be high."

"I know all about sacrifices. I'm not afraid of hard work."

"I thought the same thing. Once. Sometimes you don't realize how much something means to you until it's gone."

Hunter eyed the district attorney. "I'll think on it. Was there anything else you wanted?"

Garrett stood and moved to the doorway. "Only that I need your answer a month or two before I leave."

"When is that?"

"End of the year."

"You'll have it." Hunter ran his hand along the stubble on his jaw, his mind a sudden jumble of unanswered questions.

He stared at the empty doorway a long time after Garrett had gone through it. He wasn't at all sure how he felt about assuming the D.A.'s position, even though it would go a long way toward proving he could handle responsibility. It would also provide security for Ashley and the children. He would have to make certain sacrifices, but maybe it wasn't such a bad thing.

For now he couldn't afford to lose the job he had. He liked what he did and had no intention of being fired.

One thing was certain. Things were going to have to change if he wanted to keep his job. He had planned to start painting the house and then the barn, but he'd have to put that on hold for now. He would work harder, put in more hours at the office. He would do that and more to provide stability for Ashley.

Even though spending time away from Ashley was the last thing Hunter wanted, it was probably for the best. She was halfway through her fifth month and looked more beautiful every day. Keeping his hands off her had become damned difficult. And, frankly, he wasn't sure how much longer he could hold out.

Ashley wasn't going to play second fiddle, not like all the other nights when Hunter had brought work home and closeted himself away, almost as if he intentionally avoided her. This evening he had picked up barbecue chicken, but had barely touched it before closing himself off in his room…again. Well, she was tired of being shut out. Somehow, she would get Hunter to reveal what troubled him, and maybe in the process, ease the intense loneliness she had suffered the past few weeks.

Having finished her shower, she slipped on a gown and stood outside Hunter's bedroom, gathering her courage. She'd done her best in past weeks to respect his need to work in private, but not tonight. Without giving herself a chance to back out, she knocked, then strode inside at his invitation.

Hunter glanced up from the bed where he worked,

propped against the headboard. Her gaze centered on the top button at the waist of his jeans, which he hadn't fastened, the fabric worn white along the fly. One pant leg had a split at the knee and both hems were raveled. Not the image of an assistant district attorney, but that of a desirable and sensual man.

"Did you need something?" he asked, shuffling a stack of papers.

Her ex-husband hadn't liked for her to interrupt his work. She wondered if Hunter would get angry over this untimely intrusion. "Are you busy?"

"Not so much." He patted the side of the bed. "Come sit down." He moved several folders and a yellow legal pad to make room for her.

"I've had the impression that something's bothering you," Ashley said, circling the bed. "I thought we might talk."

"There's really nothing to say."

Things weren't going as she'd hoped. "Is it work related?"

Hunter looked at her, the creases at the corners of his eyes deepening in the shadows cast by the lamp. "Partly, but it's not anything you need be concerned with."

Disappointed by his dismissal, she clasped her hands in her lap. "Then could we talk about something else?"

Hunter settled his work in a chair, then swung his legs around to sit beside Ashley. He slid his arm around her shoulders and pulled her close to his side. "Lay down here on my bed with me and we'll talk as long as you want."

Warmth blossomed in her at his words, and she didn't hesitate to accept. "I guess maybe I should worry about your proposition, but I'll take you up on it."

He stood and lifted her, placing his knee on the mattress as he lowered her in the middle of the bed and kissed her forehead. "Believe me, I have no ulterior motive other than trying to keep you off your feet."

When he settled beside her and pulled her into his arms, she went willingly.

"Is your back still bothering you?"

She'd only mentioned her back hurting once and was surprised Hunter remembered. "Some."

He turned on his side and tugged her to face him, then began to massage her aching muscles.

Ashley groaned, enjoying the feel of his strong hand as he stroked her spine.

"Does that feel good?" he whispered in her ear.

It took all her concentration to form one word. "Heavenly."

The force of his fingers moved her closer to him until her belly settled against Hunter. When she tried to scoot away, he tightened his hold around her shoulders and whispered against her ear, "It's okay. Just relax."

And so she did, letting him work his magic on her back. It felt so good to be in his arms, to have him holding her as he had on their honeymoon.

Startled by the sudden strong kick low in her abdomen, Ashley's eyes sprung open. Her gaze locked with Hunter's. He looked as though he'd just seen a martian. "Did you feel that?"

"Yeah, was that the babies?" The hand which had earlier massaged her back moved between them to touch her stomach.

She smiled at his reaction. "Yes, that's them."

"How long has this been happening?"

"I felt some movement not long after we married, but it was like butterfly wings. It's gotten stronger since then. Sometimes it's like they're stretching and the actions are smooth and flowing, but other times it's like now and a definite kick or series of jabs.''

Hunter smiled at the hearty whack beneath his palm. ''Why didn't you tell me?''

Ashley placed her hand over his and moved it to where she felt activity from the other baby. ''I intended to, but you're always working. I wasn't sure you'd want to know.''

He frowned. ''I'm swamped and trying to dig out, but that doesn't mean I won't make time for you if it's something you believe is important.''

Hunter slipped his arm from beneath her head and scooted down on the bed, rolling Ashley onto her back. Before she knew what he planned, he laid his cheek on her tummy.

''Hunter, will you tell me about your other child?''

His hands fisted in the quilt. ''It was a long time ago. We were just sixteen. When we found out about the baby, we wanted to get married even though our folks were against it. Her folks finally convinced her to give up the baby for adoption, but then she had a miscarriage in her fourth month.''

Tears slipped down Ashley's cheeks. ''I'm sorry.''

''You know, for a long time I thought the reason my child died is because it didn't think anyone wanted it. Things had gotten so bad between Courtney and me that we could hardly talk without fighting and our parents just made things worse by deciding to keep us apart. I should have stood up to my folks, should have put my foot down when Courtney decided to give our baby up for adoption. Most of all, I regret not fighting harder for my child. I intended to raise it alone if need be, but I never got the chance to tell it. I won't repeat that mistake. Our babies will know how I feel. Do you think they can hear me?''

It took a moment before she could speak past the emotion blocking her throat. "I believe they can. I've heard of some fathers reading to their unborn babies so they'll learn their voices."

Releasing the blanket, he pressed his palm on her tummy beside his cheek and gently tapped his forefinger. "Hey, guys, listen up. It's Dad. I love you. I'll be there waiting when it's time." Then he kissed her stomach.

Ashley felt compassion for the young man that Hunter had been. She wanted to hold him, to ease his pain, but because of their positions had to be content with placing her hand on his head. She closed her eyes and savored the feel of his thick hair between her fingers. Then she knew instinctively what she had to do. Hunter had let down his guard and shared a part of himself with her. Could she do any less? "Every day with the babies something's different."

He crawled farther up the bed and pulled her back into his arms, then pressed a kiss against her temple. "Different how?"

"This past week they've been waking me during the night."

Another solid kick landed where her tummy pressed against Hunter. The lines bracketing his mouth eased, and he smiled. She'd never known him to so completely let down his guard. And the wonder she saw in his expression renewed her hope that things might work out between them after all.

When he feathered kisses along her jaw, she arched her neck to give him better access, knowing she shouldn't but unable to stop herself from wanting his touch, his mouth, his hands on her.

Ashley reminded herself that wanting Hunter to have feelings for her wouldn't necessarily make it so. Their marriage might always be exactly what it was now—nothing but an arrangement for the sake of their children where she and Hunter shared little other than a few stolen moments. Making love wouldn't change any of that. But when his lips claimed hers in a kiss that spoke of hunger long denied, she forgot everything, except Hunter.

Ashley didn't remember putting her arms around his neck, but she must have because she held him tight, wishing this moment would never end. Wanting him so much frightened her, she was finally forced to admit she didn't want him to stop. When he ended the kiss, Ashley snuggled closer to prevent him from seeing her disappointment. She pressed her cheek against him and listened as his heart kept time with hers.

He pulled her up to meet his mouth. It didn't make sense, but felt so right. Their marriage hadn't been borne out of love, but against all odds she had fallen. For now she would be content to let Hunter hold her while she remained silent. Just for a little while though, because Ashley wanted more. She wanted more than for him to come home every night because she had given him two children. She wanted him to want her, to love her.

Ashley's lips parted beneath Hunter's as his hands slid up from her waist to cup her breasts, his thumbs and forefingers making thought impossible as he kneaded her tender flesh. He trailed kisses down her throat, his whisker stubble adding to the delicious sensations spreading through her like warm butter. The whisper of his breath across her skin burned her, aroused her, convinced her she would go up in flames at any moment. Then his lips closed over the peak of her breast through her gown. She gasped and clung to him.

She couldn't draw a breath, couldn't think, couldn't feel beyond what his hands and mouth were doing. Just when she thought she couldn't bear the intensity any longer, he pulled away with a pained expression. "We can't do this, can we?"

"Dr. Rollins said it was okay at my last appointment."

He smoothed his palm over the curve of her jaw. "I don't want to hurt you."

Her chest constricted at his words. "I'll tell you if you do."

Ashley caught Hunter's arm as he lifted the hem of her gown. "Turn the light out. I don't want you to see me like this."

"But I want to see you, all of you. I've already missed so much, please let me have this." When he gave her gown another tug and pulled it over her head, she didn't try to stop him. Hunter stared at her, his unreadable features giving away none of what he felt. He touched the swell of her tummy almost reverently. Still, Ashley wished she could cover herself. "You're more beautiful than I imagined," he whispered.

His words made her heart race and she welcomed the feel of his mouth on hers, the touch of his palm as it moved to cup her breast, and the sweep of his tongue as she opened for him.

Hunter's fingers began to explore, tentative at first, then bolder as they stroked and caressed until her body hummed with need. She thought she would shatter into a million shards when he continued his assault with his mouth, but somehow she didn't.

She fumbled with the buttons on his jeans and he finally had to take over. Hunter was awesome in every respect, and she looked her fill until he pulled her against him. The feel of skin to skin made her want more, want him. Her hands brushed and stroked his chest. Then she welcomed him into her body.

Hunter took his time, drawing everything out and out

farther still until she wanted to scream. With every gasp, every sigh, he made certain he hadn't hurt her, made certain she liked what he was doing. Finally Hunter must have sensed that Ashley teetered on the edge of ecstasy, because he slid one of her legs over his hip, then made her come apart in his arms.

Later, content and exhausted, she snuggled against him and smiled when he tightened his arms around her.

"I'm sorry, Ashley," he whispered against her ear. "I tried to be gentle, but I think I might have been a little too rough. Did I hurt you?"

*Rough?* "No. It was fine." Better than fine. Hunter had been most patient in tending to her needs, doing things she'd never experienced before, taking her places she'd never been, refusing to let her hold back any part of herself.

Though Ashley hadn't planned for them to make love, she wasn't sorry, even if Hunter's tender care had made her fall helplessly in love with him. Though she was more determined than ever to make their marriage work, she couldn't help but wonder whether Hunter had married her because he had come to care for her. Or had it been only because he'd already lost one child? And would they ever find true happiness until she knew which it had been?

## Chapter Nine

Hunter hurried through the front door, glad to be home, his gaze automatically seeking Ashley. He found her asleep on the couch and bent down to kiss her. "Hi, gorgeous."

She stretched and after working at it a moment focused on him. "Hmm. Hi."

"I called you earlier and you didn't answer. Next time you go outside to check on the new kittens, would you take the cell phone so I don't worry?"

"I didn't go to the barn. I went to see Dr. Rollins."

"Was your appointment today?"

"No."

He noticed she was a little pale. Not much, but enough to alarm him. "What's wrong? Aren't you feeling okay? Is it because of last night?"

She drew a deep breath and exhaled slowly. "Dr. Rollins assured me it's probably nothing."

Hunter couldn't draw a breath. "Are you bleeding again?"

"No, not that. Contractions. I started having them about ten o'clock this morning."

He dropped to the sofa's edge beside her. "Why didn't you call me?"

"I did, but your office said you were in a meeting and had asked not to be disturbed."

Guilt washed over him in waves. He had been behind closed doors with Garrett discussing election strategies. "That never applies to you. Next time call my cell phone."

"I did. You didn't answer."

Hunter raked his fingers through his hair and muttered a curse. "I turned it off so I wouldn't be disturbed. I wasn't thinking." He wasn't used to having someone who needed to reach him for other than business reasons. "I'll have a talk with my secretary tomorrow. From now on, she'll find me when you call, no matter what."

Ashley placed her hand on his knee. "Don't be hard on her, Hunter. I didn't explain why I wanted you."

She shouldn't have had to explain. If he had been doing his duty, she would have been able to get through, Hunter thought. "What did the doctor say?"

"He did an exam to rule out premature labor and put me on a monitor for two hours."

"Dammit, I should have been with you." It didn't sit well that he'd screwed up again. Instead of taking care of Ashley like he was supposed to, he'd been talking with Garrett.

"It turned out okay."

That wasn't the point. Hunter hadn't done what he'd promised, hadn't been responsible. "Since you're home, I assume it wasn't premature labor and he stopped the contractions."

Ashley gave him a forced smile, but he had been around her long enough to know she hadn't recovered completely from her earlier ordeal. "They stopped on their own. He said they were Braxton-Hicks contractions, which are a mild muscle spasm."

"What causes them?"

She chewed her bottom lip.

"Ashley, don't keep things from me."

"Dr. Rollins said they're most common after lovemaking, but can also happen when the bladder is full. That doesn't mean what we did last night caused this to happen. Most pregnant women have them off and on the entire nine months, but they don't feel them."

"But you did which means they were pretty strong."

"I overreacted."

"No. You reacted to the information you had, same as I would have done."

"I was scared since I'm barely in my third trimester. The contractions were coming steadily every few minutes."

The tears collecting in her eyes made Hunter lift her onto his lap and hold her tight. She hadn't said it, but he knew Ashley had thought she was losing their babies. He'd let her down, and she'd faced it all alone. Hunter kissed her forehead, trying not to remember the times he had let others down and how he had felt when he'd learned Courtney had lost their baby. He never wanted Ashley to know that feeling. "Did the doctor give you any orders?"

"He said to go about our business as usual. If the contractions happen again, I'm to call him. He's being overcautious because I'm carrying twins."

"Which is what we'll be, too. From now on, you'll always know where I'm at and be able to reach me. I imagine you're hungry, so I'll go see what I can throw together." When she got off his lap, he stood. Hunter placed his hand on her shoulder. "Why don't you stay here and rest? I'll do it."

Hunter could kick himself for what had happened between them. Despite what she'd said, he blamed himself and swore the events of last night wouldn't be repeated until after the babies were born, no matter how much he might want Ashley. He didn't know how he would keep his hands off her unless he worked the long hours Garrett had suggested. Knowing that staying away from her, same as he had his family all these years, was the best thing he could do didn't sit well. He avoided his folks because he hadn't been able to forgive their part in trying to keep him from Courtney and their child. His reasons for staying away from Ashley had to do with his lack of self-control where she was concerned. He didn't want to leave her alone. But, for now, it was the best thing he could do for Ashley.

Ashley couldn't fault Hunter for being true to his word. Over the weeks since they'd made love and she'd had the scare, her calls were always put promptly through to him. He'd gone out of his way to see that she stayed off her feet as much as possible and had hired a woman who came in twice a week to cook and clean so Ashley wouldn't feel tempted. He called several times a day, had been wonderful in his concern, but something was wrong, because he'd also become distant.

Ashley ran her hands over her enlarged stomach. She couldn't blame him for not finding her desirable any longer. She was in her eighth month of pregnancy and had gained forty pounds. She felt like a blimp. Every man's fantasy. Yeah, right.

She'd wanted to have a baby for so very long and had finally gotten her wish. Not that she would ever blame her children if Hunter never desired her again. She patted her tummy and smiled, more than willing to pay any price for her precious babies.

Only she wanted Hunter, too. She longed for him to hold her as he had that night, to kiss her, to make love to her again.

If only things could go back to the way they had been that one night, when he'd touched her, found her desirable. Before her ankles had swollen to the size of coffee cans, before she spent half of each night going back and forth to the bathroom, and before she'd completely lost sight of her feet. Though it had only been a few weeks ago, it seemed like forever.

When Ashley heard Hunter's key in the door, she slid to the edge of the couch and pushed herself up to stand. Hunter closed the door behind him and glanced at her. The warmth in his eyes gave her hope as they lingered overlong on her, but then he coughed and settled several boxes of Chinese food on the table.

Her gaze traveled over the navy suit and white shirt, which contrasted sharply with his black hair and tanned complexion. The dark circles under his eyes seemed more pronounced than when she'd last seen him. Fear she might be losing him threatened to choke her. She intended to resolve it now before she fell any more in love with him, if that was possible. "I guess the honeymoon's over."

He glanced at her, a puzzled look on his face. "What did you say?"

"You heard me."

"Yes, I did, but I don't know the reasoning behind it."

"It's been weeks since you've been home and spent time with me. What am I supposed to think, Hunter?"

"What about the truth?"

"And that would be?" she asked.

"That I'm working at the office."

Disappointment almost buckled her knees. She gave him her back, not wanting him to see how much the lie hurt her. "That one was exhausted by my ex. You'll have to do better than that."

He took her arm and moved to stand in front of her. "I've told you before I'm not your ex and I won't pay for what he did. I'm really sorry you don't believe me, but I told you the truth."

She hated feeling so insecure, but this past month was like a rerun of what she'd gone through with her ex-husband before her life had fallen apart. Only now her stomach resembled a road map of stretch marks, and she was retaining water like a sponge. "I'm sorry, Hunter. I don't want to argue. I didn't mean to accuse you of anything. Could we talk? Please?"

He set his jaw and motioned her to the couch.

After Hunter had settled beside her, he asked, "What do you want to talk about?"

For the first time in a long time, Ashley was worried. Really worried. But she had to know. "I realize that in the beginning, this marriage wasn't supposed to be anything more than an arrangement for our children's sake."

"No, that's not necessarily the case. You knew I wanted it to be as close to a real marriage as possible. I wanted it to work."

She drew a deep breath and tried to calm herself, wondering if Hunter realized he had said he'd *wanted* it—past tense—instead of *want* it—present tense. So what did it mean? Had he changed his mind? What did he want now? "That's true." Still, it had never been a conventional marriage, because he'd only made love to her the one time. "What I'm getting at is, if there's someone else, another woman, I would like to know."

His blue eyes turned to ice. "Dammit, I'm working myself to death for us. There is no other woman."

Ashley sat unmoving with her hands clasped in what little lap she had left, suddenly unable to meet his gaze.

"I can't believe you really think our marriage means so little, that you mean so little to me that I would carry on with someone else while you're pregnant with my babies."

She covered her face with both hands to shut out the hurt she glimpsed in his eyes. "I don't know what I think anymore."

He tugged her hands down. "Either you believe me or you don't."

She met his gaze then and knew she'd been wrong. "No. I don't think you'd do that. I'm just feeling like a beached whale and a little insecure. No, make that a lot insecure."

"Why?" he asked, placing his palm on her stomach. "You're beautiful."

"Then why aren't you coming home until late?" *Why don't you hold me, kiss me anymore?*

"Because I'm trying to get caught up at work so that when you finally do have these babies, I can take some time off and be with you. Plus I had to run by the jail. Greg Johnson was picked up in connection with a burglary. He says he didn't do it, but they found a stolen gun in his bedroom."

"I'm sorry. I know how hard you've tried to get through to him."

"Yeah, but I didn't make it."

"But you tried, which is more than most folks would have done. I hope you're not too tired to talk about us because while you're worrying about Greg Johnson, I'm worrying about you. You've been coming home so late and by the time you feed the animals, I'm asleep. Last week I went to your bed to wait on you. You never joined me."

He looked at the toes of his shoes. "I didn't want to disturb you, so I slept on the couch."

"Oh." His answers sounded reasonable, but they didn't do anything to dispel the rejection she was feeling.

He kissed her forehead and gave her a brief hug. "I should have made sure you knew why I was working later than usual. I assumed you'd understand."

"Does your boss put in as many hours as you?"

Hunter studied her for a long minute. "More. He's there when I arrive and generally still there when I leave."

"I'm glad you're not the D.A."

He frowned, then looked away. "The work is there. Someone has to do it."

"How can they expect you to put in so many hours and still have a life? Can't they hire someone else?"

It felt as if the babies were having a soccer game in her stomach and she caught Hunter's hand and moved it over the active baby.

He smiled at the movement beneath his palm. "There's no money in the budget for an additional person."

"Will your workload get any better toward the end of the year?"

"No. I'll have to do the same amount of work in less time because of the holidays."

"But after we got married, you were bringing work home—"

"I wasn't doing my job, Ashley, not the way it's supposed to be done. I let the work slide and got called on the carpet for it. I can't afford to get fired, not with the babies on the way."

"What about after they're born?" she asked, knowing what his answer would be but needing to ask anyway.

"I'll spend as much time with them as I can, but I have to do my job. Maybe I can go in earlier and come home before they go to bed at night."

"Hunter."

"Yes."

"What about us?"

"Look, I'm doing the best I can. I thought you knew what my job was like when you married me."

"I thought I did, but I've decided I don't like your job anymore."

"I know," he said, squeezing her hand. "I've had my doubts lately, too."

"Have you ever considered going to work for your dad? It might take some of the pressure off you."

Hunter dropped her hand. "Am I the only one who believes I'm capable of doing this job?"

She sensed his withdrawal and knew she'd said something wrong. "I didn't mean you aren't."

"Dammit, I like what I do. And I'm good at it."

"I know. I just thought working with him might be an option."

Hunter jumped to his feet as if he couldn't bear to sit beside her. "I told you before that things between us are difficult. Besides, I'm happy where I am." His eyes filled with a deep sadness that tugged at her heart.

"I'm sorry I mentioned it."

He marched to the front door, then paused with his hand on the knob. "I'm going back to work."

"But you haven't eaten."

"I'll grab something on the way into town."

"Hunter, don't—"

But then he was gone, the swishing of the curtains covering the window in the door the only indication he'd been there.

It felt almost like a rerun of the argument she'd had with her ex. Only this time she had no intention of giving up and disappearing without a fight.

And Hunter's mistress wasn't a woman. It was his job

and something in the past that had come between him and his father.

Well, she had news for her husband. This time she wouldn't let a demanding job or Hunter's stupid pride tear them apart. Somehow she would find a way to save her marriage and put an end to the total lack of communication between father and son. Even if she had to go against Hunter's wishes.

"Hello, Mr. Morgan, I'm Ashley, your daughter-in-law."

The only way she could describe the look that crossed Buchanan Morgan's face was stunned disbelief. Then he smiled, and she didn't know what to make of that.

She could tell he wasn't sure what to do or say. Finally he pulled a chair from beneath the conference room table. "Please have a seat."

"I know that making an appointment and springing this news on you was a cruel trick, but I was afraid you might not see me if I told you my name and why I've come here."

He cleared his throat. "Why *are* you here? Is something wrong with Hunter?"

"No, he's fine. I wanted to introduce myself and get to know Hunter's father and my children's grandfather. Since I had a doctor's appointment today, I thought it a perfect opportunity."

His gaze swept over her, pausing momentarily on her enormous stomach. "Is it safe for you to be out in your condition?"

Ashley smiled and patted her tummy. "So long as I don't go into labor." *Or Hunter doesn't find out what I'm doing.*

He looked so panicked she felt the need to reassure him. "I'm not due for another month."

His eyes widened and his gaze once more dropped to her stomach. "Another month?"

"We're expecting twins."

"Twins? I knew about the baby, but I hadn't heard anything about twins."

Ashley kept up a stream of idle chatter while watching him come to grips with her news. "I had to take a taxi because I can't fit behind the steering wheel of my car anymore."

His expression softened. The attorney facade was no longer in evidence when he smiled. Maybe he wasn't the ogre Hunter had portrayed him to be. "Do you know if they're girls or boys or one of each?"

"No, Hunter and I want to be surprised." She placed her hand over a baby's foot or knee or elbow that raised her dress with a series of jabs. "If the way it feels means anything, I would say there's an entire football team of Morgan boys in there."

His blue eyes, so like Hunter's, lit up. "Eunice, Hunter's mother, will be beside herself. She'll probably drive you crazy with phone calls."

"I would like that. I lost both my parents in a car wreck a few years back."

"I'm sorry to hear that."

She smoothed her hands over her stomach. "I still miss them." She guessed she always would. "I confess, Mr. Morgan—"

"Call me Buck."

"Okay, Buck. There's another reason for my visit."

He raised a brow. At that moment he was an older version of Hunter. "And that would be?"

"To invite you and your wife to dinner."

He exhaled a slow breath and leaned back in his chair. "I'm not certain that's a good idea."

"Why not?"

"Have you mentioned this to Hunter?"

"No. I want to surprise him. I would like you and the rest of the family to come."

Buchanan frowned. "Eunice would like nothing better, but Hunter and I can't be in the same room without arguing."

"I'm carrying your grandchildren. I want them to have a family, and that includes grandparents. I want Sunday dinners and holidays with the whole family. The only way that's going to happen is if you and Hunter patch things up between you."

"Hunter knows where to find me."

Ashley wanted to smile at the similarities between father and son. "Why does Hunter have to be the one to make the first step?"

"Well, I don't guess it has to be him." He stood and turned away from her. "I don't know how much Hunter has told you, but there's a lot of water under the bridge."

She wasn't about to confess that Hunter had told her very little. "Will you try?"

Buck pivoted to face her. "I can't make any guarantees. Hunter is—"

"A lot like you," Ashley said. "Now I see where he gets his pride. Did he also get his stubborn determination from you?"

"Yes, I suppose he did." Buck ran his fingers along the edge of his polished desk, then glanced at her. "Why didn't you call Hunter's mother about this?"

Ashley smiled. "I can't make Hunter do anything he doesn't want and suspected I'd have a better chance of convincing you if I came here rather than to your wife."

Buck roared with laughter. "All right, we'll come."

"Great. We'll see you Friday night at seven?"

Ashley didn't fool herself. Chances were one dinner wouldn't make Buck forget or Hunter forgive himself. But then the odds of her conceiving hadn't been all that great, either.

Hunter hurried into the house, worrying that Ashley's cryptic message to come home and his brother's car in the driveway meant something was wrong. Voices came to him from the kitchen and he quickened his steps, then screeched to a stop when he saw his father seated at the head of the table as if he belonged there. His mother sat beside Buck, her smile strained. Next to her was Jared and Lauren who both looked guilty. And across the table sat Ashley smiling as if she'd just handed him a prize.

"Hunter," she said, struggling to gain her feet.

He hurried to help her. "What's going on? Why is my family here?"

"Hunter, please," she whispered. "I invited them to dinner." She drew him to the chair beside her. "I wanted to get everyone together so we could get to know each other."

"I don't think this is a good—"

"Just dinner. Then we'll see where we go from there. It will be fun. You'll see."

As usual, he couldn't deny her. "Don't expect miracles. There are things you don't know."

She placed her hand on his knee. "Everything will work out if you'll just let it."

He feared nothing good would come of this, but he wouldn't disappoint her by ruining her efforts.

"Hunter," Eunice said as she passed the salad around the table, "Ashley is exactly what you've needed all these years."

Hunter considered his mother's words. Just the prospect of needing Ashley unsettled him. She had made him feel things he hadn't felt comfortable examining, things he'd chalked up to his need to protect her. Ashley *was* kind and forgiving. And far too trusting and naive for her own good. Granted, she was a lot of things, but she couldn't heal their family over dinner or erase his troubled past.

Jared and Buck managed to carry the dinner conversation which inevitably turned to politics. Hunter decided to keep his opinions to himself since he and his father had never agreed anyway.

"You know, Ashley, I'm glad you two decided to get married." Buck cut into his steak. "Great timing with the babies coming. Very advantageous for Hunter's future."

Ashley glanced at Hunter, then at Buck. "I don't understand. How could our marrying be good for Hunter's job?"

Jared cleared his throat. "Dinner is great. Isn't it, Lauren?"

When Lauren didn't answer right away, Jared nudged her arm with his elbow. "Yes. Very good."

Eunice Morgan frowned at her husband. "Buchanan, you promised."

Buck sputtered. "What did I do?"

Ashley looked at each person around the table. "Why do I feel as if I'm the only one who isn't in on some big secret?"

Buck swore under his breath. "She doesn't know?"

Hunter wanted to be angry with his father, but as usual the blame was his for putting off the inevitable. "No. I haven't told her."

Eunice gave him a hard look. "Why not? It affects her, too."

"I know. I had planned to tell her later."

"Hunter Morgan, that sounds like something your father would do," Eunice said.

The last thing Hunter wanted was to be compared to

Buck, but more than that he didn't want to have to tell Ashley like this. He put his arm around the back of her chair. "Garrett Tyler is leaving. Unless someone challenges me, it looks like I'll fill the vacancy."

Her eyes widened. "As district attorney."

"Yeah."

"H-how long have you known about this, Hunter?" she asked, her voice dropping to a whisper.

He didn't want to tell her for fear she might never forgive him, but he hadn't ever lied to her. And he wasn't about to start now. "Since before we married."

She chewed her bottom lip. "You knew when you proposed?"

"Yeah. I knew."

She stared at her hands clasped on top of her stomach. After a long moment, she pushed away from the table and struggled to stand. "Excuse me."

"I didn't know," Buck said. "I'm sorry."

Hunter lunged to his feet, knocking his chair over in his haste. "Are you, Dad?"

"That's enough!" Eunice Morgan leapt to her feet. "I love you both, but this has gone on long enough. You're not resolving anything. And this time you've upset Ashley."

Only then did Hunter realize Ashley had gotten away from him. He had to find her, explain why he hadn't told her about the possibility of him becoming the next district attorney. And when he did tell her, he didn't want an audience. "It might be best if you all left."

Eunice circled the table to hug him. "You've got your work cut out for you. If I were Ashley, I would stay mad at you for at least a month."

Lauren gave him a concerned smile. "Call if you need us."

Jared slapped Hunter on the back. "She'll come around…eventually."

Buck stood at the end of the table, a frown on his face. "I didn't know. I would never have mentioned it if I had."

Eunice took Buck's arm. "Come on. Let's go. Hunter and Ashley need time alone to work this out."

Hunter wasn't at all sure time would be enough to fix things between him and Ashley. He spent most days in court arguing cases, providing evidence which would sway a jury's decision. This time, he had no defense. But he had to try, because he didn't know what he'd do without Ashley.

Hunter found her in her bedroom staring out the window into the night. He wanted to hold her, but doubted she would welcome his touch. "Ashley—"

"Is that why you married me?"

"No. The election had nothing to do with my reasons." When he placed a hand on her shoulder, she shrugged it off. He let his arm drop to his side. "You have to believe me."

She turned to face him. "Why didn't you tell me?"

"I intended to."

"When? After you were sworn in? Did you actually think I would welcome the news? I hardly see you now. And you told me the D.A. works longer hours than you. When will you have time to see the babies or me? Or did you plan to make time? Is this position more important than your family?"

He swore under his breath. "Of course I'll make time for you and the children. Do you really think I care so little that I wouldn't?"

"I don't know what to think anymore. At one time I thought if I tried maybe things would work out, but now—"

"It will work," he said, wanting to yell so maybe she'd listen.

Ashley faced him. "How can it when you're never here?"

"I'm trying, Ashley. Dammit, I'm trying." He reached for her hands, wanting her to understand. But he didn't think it best to tell her he stayed away because he feared making love to her would cause a reoccurrence of her having contractions. "There's so much to be done before Garrett leaves, before the babies come."

Again, she stepped away from his touch. "Is that what you're offering our children? A life of empty promises? Will they always be second or third or fourth in your life, getting whatever time you have left after all your job commitments are fulfilled? They'll get lost in the shuffle of your paperwork, and you won't notice. This has nothing to do with me or the babies. It's all about proving yourself, isn't it?"

His insides twisted into a hard knot. She was right. He'd thought only of showing everyone, including his father, that he had changed, that they had been wrong about him not being able to do the job. "Ashley, I didn't—"

"I've done everything I know to do. I'd hoped you would come around. But you haven't. And I can't do this anymore. I can't. I won't."

"What do you mean?"

She wiped at the tears that streamed down her cheeks. "I'm leaving you."

"Look, I understand you're upset with me because I didn't ask your opinion on the D.A.'s position. And I admit I wanted to show Buck I was responsible, but I think—"

"Your job and what's between you and your dad has nothing to do with my decision to leave."

"Then what?" he asked.

She inhaled a deep breath. "I want my children to know they will *always* come first. And I want to come first, too. That's something I don't believe you can do."

"I can. I will."

"At one time, I thought you could. But you're too busy trying to be perfect to make time for me. You can't build a future with me while you're clinging to the past. I don't think—"

She gasped then lifted her wide eyes to his.

"Ashley, what's wrong."

"I think my water just broke."

Hunter's children were about to be born. If anything happened to Ashley or them, he would be to blame. He should have told her about Garrett's plans a long time ago. But he hadn't wanted her to worry. Now his silence had put her and his babies in danger.

He took a deep breath, moved closer to her hospital bed and caught Ashley's hand. She pulled it back. "One of the baby's vital signs is a little low. The doctors think it best to do a C-section."

Tears pooled in her eyes, and when he tried to kiss her forehead, she turned away. "You can go now, Hunter. You don't need to stay."

"I want to be with you, Ashley."

"No, I can do this by myself."

Hunter tried not to think of her rejection as he tied the gown a nurse had given him to wear. Everything was happening too fast, and he was having trouble drawing air into his lungs.

An alarm sounded. "One of the babies is in distress. We need to go." The doctor who had barked this information sprinted from the room as the nurses prepared Ashley to follow.

Hunter hurried after the team of staff and nurses wheeling Ashley away at a run. One of the nurses caught his arm. "You can go as far as the double doors, Mr. Morgan, but you won't be allowed in surgery."

"I have to go with her. I need to be with her. I promised."

"Our primary concern is getting the babies delivered."

Hunter felt his place was at Ashley's side, but he understood the reasoning. He jogged until he came alongside Ashley. "Ashley, honey."

She looked at him with eyes so full of pain it nearly sent him to his knees. Then she turned away for the second time.

His chest tightened. "Ashley?"

Hunter's steps faltered and he stood watching until the nurses disappeared around a corner with Ashley.

And suddenly, he realized it was all too late. His reasons for not telling her about the D.A. position were no longer important. The woman he had sworn to protect and do right by was in danger. So were his children. And it was all his fault.

Even if Ashley could one day find it in her heart to forgive him, he wasn't at all sure he would ever be able to forgive himself.

He had tried so hard to prove himself worthy. Yet he had failed the one person who mattered to him above all others.

# Chapter Ten

After what seemed a lifetime, a nurse strode toward Hunter. Her serious expression made him think things hadn't gone well.

Hunter felt sick, but bolted from the chair. "Is Ashley okay?"

"The doctor is finishing up with your wife. It will be a while before she's in recovery where you can see her."

His heart thundered in his ears. "And the babies?"

"You have two beautiful sons."

Hunter's knees buckled and he landed on the edge of a chair.

She placed a hand on his shoulder. "Are you okay?"

"No, uh, yeah. I...I don't know. I'm...I'm..."

She nodded. "The oldest one weighs almost five pounds and is doing fine, breathing on his own. The other, the second born, weighs about four pounds. He's having some respiratory problems, so we put him on a ventilator."

"Ventilator?" Hunter asked, not liking the fear he heard in his voice.

"Yes. It helps him to breathe until the steroids we've started develop his lungs enough so he can do it on his own."

Hunter understood the severity of the situation, but needed to know what they were up against. "That will happen, won't it? I mean, the ventilator is only temporary?"

"It should be unless there are unforeseen complications. The doctors will talk to you when they finish with the babies."

The pounding of Hunter's heart filled his ears. "I want to see my children," he said, pushing himself up on shaky legs.

"They're in the neonatal unit."

"Why the difference in their sizes?" he asked, following her down the hall.

"It's not uncommon for the stronger baby to take all the nourishment from another fetus. Sometimes one child doesn't develop at all and often will disappear in the early stages of pregnancy. In your case, one baby is underdeveloped."

She pushed through a set of double doors. "This section of the neonatal unit is the growers and feeders. They're babies that are underweight—not critical—but we want to observe them." She pointed to a tiny plastic cart to the left. "That is your healthy son. As you can see, he's doing fine and hasn't required any type of breathing assistance. In a few minutes you can come back and visit with him. But first I'll take you to the critical care section of the neonatal unit to see your other son."

The nurse's words didn't alarm Hunter as much as what she hadn't said. He glanced once more at the cart, alarmed at how small it was. His healthy son's cries of discontent filled the room, drawing Hunter. He wanted to go to his son, hold him, love him, do all the things a proud new father would do. But the nurse's touch on Hunter's shoulder reminded him that his other child, the smaller one, the one in distress, needed him, too.

With a whispered promise to return as soon as he could, Hunter followed the nurse down the hall until she paused at a large window. Row after row of evenly spaced bassinets filled the room washed with light.

"That one there—first row straight ahead—is yours. Before you go in, you need to scrub."

Hunter's throat tightened as he stared at her, seeking an answer to his unspoken question, the one he couldn't bring himself to ask for fear of what she'd say. Finally, she left him to scrub and pull on another sterile gown.

He shouldered his way through the double doors and stepped inside the room. The strong scent of antiseptic hung in the warm air as time stood suspended in the windowless area. Equipment and monitors which would alert the staff to the slightest drop in a baby's vital signs beeped, clicked and buzzed.

Afraid yet unable to hold back, he hurried to his son. His steps faltered when he saw his child was no longer than his own forearm and not as big around. A stocking cap covered the tiny head that was smaller than Hunter's fist.

The books he'd read had prepared him for many things, but not for the rush of unconditional love that came when he looked into the innocent face of his child for the first time. The baby's size and helpless vulnerability tugged at his heartstrings. Hunter had never felt such an intense need to protect, something he hadn't been able to do fifteen years ago. He couldn't change what had happened back then. Now things were different. He was different.

His gaze locked on a tube taped to his baby's mouth. The other end connected to a machine he thought to be a ventilator. It made a rhythmic whooshing sound that matched the rise and fall of his son's chest where two white circular pads stood out in stark contrast to the blue translucence of his skin. Clamps and colored wires ran from the dots to another apparatus with a digital display.

A doctor crossed the room and paused beside the incubator, checking the equipment, then making a note on a chart.

Hunter drew a long breath and faced him. "How is he?"

The physician settled the chart on a metal shelf beneath the tiny bed and pulled off his rubber gloves. "He's doing great. We put him on the ventilator, and his blood gasses are good. He's a gutsy kid, a real fighter. We'll slowly wean him off the vent as soon as we can. I can't say for sure how long that will take. It depends on how he does each time we back the machine off a little. But with the way he's responding now, I don't see why he won't come out of here in a month, barring any complications."

The knot in Hunter's gut eased somewhat until an alarm split the silence and the doctor was gone, rushing to join two nurses at a bed across the room. He stood paralyzed, unable to look away from the numb helplessness and desolation etched on the faces of the baby's parents as they watched the doctor work to save their child.

Hunter found a tall stool and pulled it alongside his son's bed. After sliding onto the seat, he counted every finger and toe until the tears that blurred his vision made the chore impossible. He scooted closer and leaned forward, bracing his elbows on his knees as he pressed one palm against the side of the clear plastic enclosing his child. "I don't know if you can hear me or even understand what I'm saying, but I'm…I'm your daddy."

He swallowed past the tightness in his throat. "I don't want you worrying that since we have another son who is bigger and you're so tiny that we won't want you." Hunter wiped the wetness from his eyes. "I know what it's like to think that because things didn't turn out the way we expected that you're a disappointment. You're not. As far as I'm concerned, you're everything I could want in a son...more than I ever dared hope for. More than I deserve. I want to take you and your brother home where we can be a family, a real family. I'll be there for you. Always," he said in a voice that wavered. "And I'll never put my career first, never make you question if you're loved."

Hunter drew a ragged breath and continued. "I've never had the chance to be a dad before and may not always do things right, but together we'll figure it out. I love you, son. No matter what happens, no matter what you may one day do, I will always love you. Even when you make mistakes. And rather than sending you away, we'll work together to resolve our differences."

"Hunter?"

He glanced over his shoulder to find his father dressed in a sterile gown and mask. Hunter had never known him to look so humble in all his life.

Buck moved closer, his gaze lowering to the infant who more resembled a doll than a real baby. His dad put his hand on Hunter's shoulder. "After we left your house, your mother got worried because Ashley had been so upset. When you still didn't answer the phone after she'd tried for most of the night, she called the hospital and found Ashley had been admitted. I'm sorry, Hunter. I feel responsible."

"It's not your fault. If anyone is to blame, it's me. I should have told her." He recalled his mother's words and how she had given them all hell at dinner. "Where's Mom?"

"Out in the waiting room. They'd only let one of us

come in. I wanted to apologize for what happened at dinner.''

"It wasn't you. I should have told Ashley months ago. What got into Mom at dinner? She never raises her voice like that."

"You don't understand," Buck said. "We've torn your mother apart with our arguing. It's time we call a truce. You, Ashley and your babies need the support of the whole family."

Hunter couldn't believe what he'd heard.

Buck gave him a questioning look. "What you said just now about loving him even when he makes mistakes. Do you think I didn't love you?''

"Yeah, I did."

"I've always been proud of you though I never said anything. I guess I figured you should know how I felt. I'm sorry now that I never said it."

"I didn't know," Hunter said. "I wish I had."

"I may have been too hard on you. You weren't like your brother and maybe I did go a little overboard sometimes, but you always had to do things your way. You'd been in minor trouble off and on, but nothing serious until your girlfriend came up pregnant. That's when I realized I had to do something. So I sent you to that private school. I felt like I had to before you ruined your life. You never listened to me. I hoped that maybe someone else could reach you were I had failed."

Though Hunter doubted Buck would ever understand how he'd felt about Courtney and the baby, he finally realized that what his father said was true. The determination he had learned because Buck was so tough on him is what had made him a good attorney. The experience he had learned while rebelling had helped him know how to reach troubled kids from dysfunctional families and those who'd made mistakes, same as he'd done. He wanted to reach these kids before they were brought into court in handcuffs. It also made Hunter realize the importance of spending time with his own children, teaching them with a loving hand.

He turned back to his youngest child. "Would you do me a favor, Buck?"

"You name it."

"Will you stay here with him while I check on my other boy and find out if Ashley is in recovery yet? It may seem foolish, but he's so tiny, so helpless. I can't leave him by himself right now. I need him to know we're here, that he's not alone." Hunter also needed to make sure his other child was doing all right. And he ached to see Ashley, his wife, the woman he loved.

Hunter stilled. He loved her. How stupid had he been for it to take something like this for him to acknowledge that fact? He needed to go to her, say the words, make sure she knew how he felt. Maybe then the tightness in his chest would ease.

He leaned close to the enclosed bed. "This is your grandpa. He's going to stay with you while I go see your brother." And your mom. Hunter placed his palm on the warm plastic, then coughed to clear the emotion from his throat. "Thanks, Buck—err, Dad. I... Thanks."

It was Hunter who pulled Ashley from the darkness surrounding her, holding her firmly in its grasp.

She fought the deep timbre of his voice, wanted to sink deeper into the blessed numbness of oblivion a little longer. But a spark of concern turned to fear as her mind slowly cleared.

*Her babies.*

Ashley forced her eyes open and had to blink several times before she could focus on Hunter, who stood leaning over her. She'd never been so glad to see anyone in her whole life. She thought to smile, to ease the concern that puckered his brow, but memories of the night's events came to her in a rush.

The man to whom she had entrusted her heart, her children's future, had betrayed her.

The sharp pain in her abdomen dimmed in comparison to the ache of her broken heart.

"Mrs. Morgan," the nurse said, giving Ashley a reason to turn away from Hunter, to momentarily shut out his deceit. She would sort through everything later after she'd found out about her children. The pink and purple blotches on the nurse's smock blurred as Ashley blinked away the tears that threatened. "My babies?" Her dry throat made her words come out a raspy croak.

"They're in the neonatal unit," Hunter said, drawing her attention back to him. He squeezed her hand. "I just came from there."

"I want to see them."

The nurse patted her arm. "You've got to stay here a while longer. When you're ready to go to your room, your husband can take you by the nursery if you'd like."

"I want to go now."

"I'm sorry. Hospital policy," the nurse said as she moved to her next patient in the crowded recovery room.

Ashley turned to Hunter, her sudden fear and concern overriding her anger at his actions. "Are they okay?"

He opened his mouth to respond when she interrupted him. "I want the truth, Hunter."

"One is big and loud. He weighs almost five pounds and is doing fine. He reminds me a lot of my dad." Hunter smiled, but it slowly faded. "The other one is under four pounds. H-he's having a little trouble."

"Trouble?" she repeated. "What do you mean? What kind of trouble?"

"They're giving him steroids for his lungs and have him on a ventilator to help him breathe. The doctor said this is common with pre-term births. But he's optimistic and believes that barring complications, everything should be fine."

Tears clouded her vision. It was all her fault. She had failed her babies. She had gone into labor early. She was to blame.

She scrubbed at her eyes with the heels of her hands. She tried to think of something the doctor had ordered which she had failed to do, but couldn't recall a single thing. Though logic told her she had done everything she could, her heart disagreed. Her body had betrayed her as surely as Hunter had. She didn't know if she would ever be able to forgive herself...or him.

"I need to see them."

"I don't think they're going to let you out of here for a while yet. And there's some things I need to explain."

Ashley closed her eyes, wanting to hear the words that would set everything to rights. She couldn't bear the thought she had fallen in love with a man who had married her only to secure his position as the next district attorney. And though she needed Hunter at her side during the challenge ahead, she would not depend on him. From now on, she would face everything alone. "I need to see my babies. Until I know they're okay, I can't think about anything else."

The lines bracketing his mouth deepened. "All right. I'll go find your doctor."

Ashley watched Hunter approach the nurse. It didn't matter what the doctor said. If she had to belly crawl across the floor and sneak out of recovery, she would. She needed to see for herself that her babies were all right.

She also wanted to put off the confrontation with Hunter. Learning why he had married her had been painful enough. With her babies in the neonatal unit, Ashley didn't think she had the strength to withstand hearing him say the words.

For now she would hold the fragmented pieces of her heart together as best she could and focus only on helping her babies grow strong so they could all go home.

*Home.* What she and Hunter had shared for a brief time before he had become consumed by his work had been the loving home she had always wanted to give her children. Though she knew Hunter loved their babies, Ashley wasn't at all sure she could go back to living with him knowing he didn't care for her.

And he never had.

"Do you want to rest before seeing our youngest son?"

"No, I'm fine," Ashley said, holding her stomach as she leaned forward and looked through the window into what Hunter had explained was the critical care section of the neonatal unit. Her breath hitched. "Hunter, is that your mother and father?"

"Yes," he said, circling the wheelchair. "They've come here to support us because of you."

"What do you mean?" she asked as he knelt in front of her.

"Dad and I have both always been incredibly stubborn. We each wanted the other to see our side of things. You were right when you said you and I couldn't have a future with me living in the past. I think the same is true with my relationship with my father. He's not perfect, but then neither am I. I think in some ways I was afraid to face him for fear of failing once again to be the kind of son he wants, just like I've been scared to tell you some things about me.''

''You don't need—''

''I have to do this because I don't want to wonder if when you find out you'll leave.'' Hunter raked a hand through his hair, trying to formulate the words to reveal the sins of his past to the woman he loved. ''When I was a teenager, I did all kinds of things to get attention, spray-painting graffiti on buildings, busting out windows and stealing hubcaps. Well, you get the picture. I felt like Buck paid more attention to his political career than me and decided to change that. Looking back, I can't believe I was that dumb. Buck couldn't understand why I was doing all those things and yelling didn't do any good. After this went on for several years, I got caught painting graffiti at the high school field house. It was pretty graphic and got the whole town's attention. Not long after that my girlfriend discovered she was pregnant. We didn't plan for it to happen. After she miscarried, Buck shipped me off to a private school. I blamed him for my life seemingly falling apart for a long time. Finally I understood what I'd cost him. You see, he was up for a federal judgeship and my girlfriend Courtney was one of his colleagues' daughter. Her dad held what I'd done over Buck's head, threatening to tell everyone that Buck couldn't control a courtroom because he couldn't restrain me, until he withdrew from the race and from politics. It was all my fault.''

''You're wrong. Your father is responsible for his actions, not you. He withdrew because of his own reasons. Besides, you were just a kid.''

''I was old enough to know better.''

''So, this is why you've been working yourself to death, trying to be Mr. Perfect?''

"Yeah."

"Did you really think I would change my opinion of you because of this?"

"A lot of folks can't forget. I was afraid to risk it."

"Hunter, parents don't expect their children to be perfect. Neither do wives."

"You amaze me. You were able to see everything so clearly and took the bull by the horns by inviting my family to dinner." Hunter placed one hand on her knee. "You gave Dad and me two very good reasons to let go of the past."

"My dinner was only supposed to bring you together so you could talk things out."

"It worked," he said, catching her hand and pressing a kiss on her palm.

Ashley warned herself not to read anything into his kiss.

He released her hand and exhaled a slow breath. "Look, Ashley, I know you're mad at me, and I don't expect anything I say now to change that. I can't undo the past. Lord knows I wish I could, but I want you to stay, to give me another chance."

"Hunter, I don't see how—"

"I'm not taking the D.A. position."

"But I thought—"

"I know I should have talked it all over with you, but I didn't want you to worry."

"I wouldn't—"

He pressed his fingertip against her lips. "You would have worried."

"Maybe a little." It irritated her to admit he was right. She would have worried. She wanted to accept she had been wrong about Hunter, but could she believe him? "What made you change your mind?"

"You helped me realize what's really important."

"And that would be?"

"Our marriage, our babies and our family," he said, leaning forward to press a kiss against her forehead. "I didn't want the job. I never did, not really, but when Garrett told me Dad had questioned whether I could handle it, well, that made me determined to show him. It's not important, not anymore."

Ashley couldn't believe her ears. "When did you decide this?"

"Tonight," he said, flashing her his rogue's smile. "I did a lot of thinking while pacing outside the delivery room."

"But if you don't take the district attorney position, what will you do?"

"I don't know. I could go into practice with my dad. Or I could establish my own firm. I haven't given it much thought because I've been too busy worrying about you and the babies. You're the most important thing in my life, you and my sons. Will you give me another chance?"

Ashley stared at her clenched hands, not sure she could trust herself to make an unbiased decision with Hunter this close. How could she when she loved him more than life itself? He was her next breath, her life, and he had been for some time. But she knew from experience that controlling men often made rash promises to turn the tables in their favor, promises they had no intention of keeping. "Hunter, as much as I would like to believe you, I don't—"

"Ashley, baby, I know I messed up, and it will take a long time to undo that. I'm not asking for more than you can give, but I can't stand the thought of losing you. As scared as I was that something might happen to the babies, the thought of having to face tomorrow without you is ten times worse."

The remorse in his eyes tugged at her heart. She wanted to stay, to make things work, because she loved him, but wasn't sure she would survive another betrayal. ''I don't think this is a good time—''

''Ashley, I'm as close to my knees as I can get. Do you want me to beg you? I will if that's what you want.''

When he took hold of both arms of the wheelchair and shifted his weight as if to lower the other knee to the ground, Ashley grabbed his arm. ''Hunter, don't. You don't have to beg. Please. All I've ever wanted is for you to love me.''

''I do love you.''

Tears pooled in her eyes and she blinked as she met his gaze. ''Hold me, please.''

Hunter cupped her face in his hands and brushed his lips over hers. ''My pleasure.'' With that he pulled her into his arms and settled her head in the curve of his shoulder.

He pulled back and dried her cheeks with the pads of his thumbs. ''You are the best thing that's ever happened to me.''

''I know,'' she said with a teasing grin.

''And so modest. No wonder I love you.''

Ashley's heart skipped a beat. ''I love you, too.''

''I never intended for this to happen between us,'' Hunter said, one corner of his mouth lifting in a smile. ''When I learned about the mix-up at the clinic, I initially thought I might sue. But now I think I'll send them a thank-you note.''

His eyes darkened when he leaned forward and kissed her. She parted her lips to allow him access, accepting the steady heat of promise, the sweep of enduring love.

As his heart pounded beneath her palm and Hunter broke the kiss, Ashley cast aside all her doubts and fears. When he pressed his lips against her temple and pulled her into the strength of his embrace, she relaxed against him.

She knew without hesitancy or question the shelter of his arms was where she always wanted to be. It was her haven, her home. No matter what he did or where they lived, Hunter was her husband, the man she loved. "What do you say we go inside and see the rest of our family, Dad?"

seemed to HUNTER cradled his smallest son in the crook of her

# *Epilogue*

Hunter cradled his smallest son in the crook of his arm
as he helped Ashley up the porch steps.

The door opened to Hunter's mother. "Come on inside
out of the cold."

They made their way into the living room where his dad
sat in a rocking chair before a roaring fire, a Santa cap on
his head and their dog, Sheeba, asleep at his feet. In his
arms, Hunter's oldest son who had gone home three weeks
earlier.

"Can you handle one more?" Hunter asked as he settled
the smaller baby in his father's free arm while Hunter's
oldest child squirmed in the other, drawing Sheeba's attention. After getting up to check out the new arrival, the dog
settled down to resume her own nap.

His dad beamed. "I handled you, didn't I?"

"Yeah, you did." Hunter helped Ashley remove her coat
and hung it in the closet.

Lauren carried a tray of hot cocoa from the kitchen and

offered a cup to Jared, who lounged on the couch beside Hunter's boss, Garrett Tyler.

Hunter's heart warmed at the surprise on Ashley's face as she stared at the huge Christmas tree his family had decorated while he and Ashley had gone to bring their youngest home. The pile of presents beneath the tree had doubled since they'd left and he turned to his mother. With a nod of his head toward the tree, he asked, "Where did the other gifts come from?"

His mom smiled. "Your father and I have waited a long time for grandchildren. Humor us."

Garrett laughed. "I never did hear what names you two finally decided on."

Ashley and Hunter joined Jared and Garrett on the couch and accepted a cup of hot cocoa from Lauren.

"Since you agreed to be their godfather, you need to visit often enough that you can tell them apart. The loud one is Parker Buchanan, after my dad," Hunter said.

"And the littlest is Phillip Hunter after my dad and Hunter," Ashley said with a smile.

Hunter grimaced. "Ashley wanted to hang a junior on him, but I wouldn't let her. I don't mind him having Hunter as a middle name, but I want him to be his own person, not feel as if he has to prove himself for any reason."

Jared stood, then took Lauren's hand and raised the cup in his other. "I would like to make a toast. To the Morgan boys and those that will follow next year."

Hunter laughed at the panic in Ashley's brown eyes. "We're so worn out from shuffling back and forth between these two—"

"Get used to it," Eunice said with a grin. "You've only just begun."

"Yeah, well, as much as we would like more children, I don't see any more in our immediate future." Hunter leaned to whisper in Ashley's ear, "Of course, it probably wouldn't take much for you to convince me otherwise."

She blushed and pinched his arm.

"Actually," Jared continued, "I meant Lauren and me. We're going to have a baby."

A buzz of congratulations and hugs followed that announcement. Hunter couldn't help but be thankful things had turned out as they had.

At Hunter's questioning look, Jared said, "After Lauren's fertilization failed, we had decided to adopt. We thought the problem was my low sperm count, but then they decided maybe it was a combination of that and Lauren's off-and-on again ovulation problems. Lauren's doctor had warned us that once the stress of trying to conceive is gone, she might end up getting pregnant. He was right. He has other couples this same thing has happened to."

Buck allowed his wife to take Phillip from him. "This is wonderful. We're finally going to have a houseful of grandchildren. I couldn't be happier. You know, Hunter, I never did hear how you and Ashley met."

*Some things are best left unsaid.* "Well, Dad, it's a long story. Just let me say it was love at first sight. We both decided we wanted children and that's all there was to it."

"Whatever the reason, I'm glad everything has worked out." Buck's gaze went to Jared and Lauren. "For everybody."

Garrett stood and made his way to Hunter. "I'm sorry you decided not to take my place as D.A., but after seeing all this, I can certainly understand why."

"How much longer will you be in Hale?" Ashley asked.

"My car's packed. When I leave here, I'm hitting the highway."

Hunter shook Garrett's hand. "I hope you find what you're looking for."

"Oh, I've found it. I just can't have it."

The emptiness in Garrett's eyes reminded Hunter of how he'd felt when he thought he had lost Ashley. He put an arm around her, needing once again to remind her of his love. "Maybe things have changed."

Garrett shoved his hands in his blue jean pockets. "It's complicated." He strode to the door and paused before leaving. "Take care of those babies. I'll keep in touch."

When the door closed behind Garrett, Buck stood and handed Parker to Ashley. "Did Garrett say you've decided not to take the D.A. position?"

"Yeah, I turned it down." Hunter watched his father's reaction to the news and was surprised at his silence. "Dad, I was wondering if you might want another partner?"

"Do you mean you'll come to work with me and Jared?" Buck asked, hope in his voice.

"That's what it means. You need to know I won't do divorces or custody cases. But I'll make a hell of a juvenile attorney."

"What?"

"I want to represent troubled teens, see if I can reach them where the system has failed. I think I have the necessary credentials. I convinced Greg Johnson, a troubled teen, to give the system a chance. He testified that the stolen gun they found in his bedroom belonged to his friend, who had asked Greg to hang on to it. The burglary charge against Greg has been dropped. He's back in school and doing great."

"When do you want to start?" Buck asked, his smile widening.

"Garrett's replacement brought in someone and I've already shown him the ropes. But I want to spend a couple of weeks with Ashley and the babies. How about two weeks?"

"Morgan, Morgan & Morgan. Has a nice sound," Buck said, moving out of the way so Eunice could give Phillip to Hunter.

Hunter smiled at the big red bows affixed to the end of the twin cradles he'd made. Having his family around would take some getting used to, but it was a change he more than looked forward to. Almost as much as he looked forward to being able to make love to Ashley again.

He noticed mistletoe hanging from the ceiling and brushed a kiss across her lips. "I wanted to give you a special Christmas gift, but we've got another week or two to wait to get the doctor's okay." He pulled a ring from his jacket pocket and slipped it on the third finger of her right hand. "Until then, this will have to do."

Ashley stared at the two blue topaz stones twinkling in the gold mother's ring, then met his gaze. "Oh, Hunter. It's beautiful."

When Phillip began to fuss, he rocked his son in the crook of his arm. "The jeweler assured me we can add more stones to it."

She settled Parker on her shoulder. "Do you really want more?"

"Oh, yes," he said with a grin. "This time I'll be there for their conception and every day after."

Hunter leaned toward Ashley and kissed her, telling her without words that she would never again have reason to doubt his love or his dedication to his family.

Because of her and the love they shared, he had become a family man. And he wouldn't have had it any other way.

\* \* \* \* \*

**You've shared love, tears and laughter.**

**Now share your love of reading—**

**give your daughter Silhouette Romance® novels.**

*Silhouette*®
*Where love comes alive*™

Visit Silhouette at www.eHarlequin.com

SRMAD

*Silhouette presents an exciting
new continuity series:*

**When a royal family rolls out the red carpet
for love, power and deception, will their
lives change forever?**

**The saga begins in April 2002 with:**

## The Princess Is Pregnant!

**by Laurie Paige (SE #1459)**

**May: THE PRINCESS AND THE DUKE by Allison Leigh
(SE #1465)**

**June: ROYAL PROTOCOL by Christine Flynn
(SE #1471)**

Be sure to catch all nine Crown and Glory stories: the first three appear in
Silhouette Special Edition, the next three continue in Silhouette Romance
and the saga concludes with three books in Silhouette Desire.

---

And be sure not to miss more royal stories,
from Silhouette Intimate Moments'

# Romancing
# the Crown,

**running January through December.**

*Silhouette*®

™ *Where love comes alive*™

*Available at
your favorite
retail outlet.*

Visit Silhouette at www.eHarlequin.com

SSECAG

If you enjoyed what you just read,
then we've got an offer you can't resist!

# Take 2 bestselling
# love stories FREE!
# Plus get a FREE surprise gift!

**Clip this page and mail it to Silhouette Reader Service™**

**IN U.S.A.**
3010 Walden Ave.
P.O. Box 1867
Buffalo, N.Y. 14240-1867

**IN CANADA**
P.O. Box 609
Fort Erie, Ontario
L2A 5X3

**YES!** Please send me 2 free Silhouette Romance® novels and my free surprise gift. After receiving them, if I don't wish to receive anymore, I can return the shipping statement marked cancel. If I don't cancel, I will receive 6 brand-new novels every month, before they're available in stores! In the U.S.A., bill me at the bargain price of $3.15 plus 25¢ shipping and handling per book and applicable sales tax, if any*. In Canada, bill me at the bargain price of $3.50 plus 25¢ shipping and handling per book and applicable taxes**. That's the complete price and a savings of at least 10% off the cover prices—what a great deal! I understand that accepting the 2 free books and gift places me under no obligation ever to buy any books. I can always return a shipment and cancel at any time. Even if I never buy another book from Silhouette, the 2 free books and gift are mine to keep forever.

215 SEN DFNQ
315 SEN DFNR

| | | |
|---|---|---|
| Name | (PLEASE PRINT) | |
| Address | Apt.# | |
| City | State/Prov. | Zip/Postal Code |

\* Terms and prices subject to change without notice. Sales tax applicable in N.Y.
\*\* Canadian residents will be charged applicable provincial taxes and GST.
  All orders subject to approval. Offer limited to one per household and not valid to current Silhouette Romance® subscribers.
  ® are registered trademarks of Harlequin Enterprises Limited.

SROM01                                                    ©1998 Harlequin Enterprises Limited

Silhouette Romance introduces tales of
enchanted love and things beyond explanation
in the new series

# Soulmates

Couples destined for each other are brought
together by the powerful magic of love....

A precious gift brings
## A HUSBAND IN HER EYES
by Karen Rose Smith (on sale March 2002)

Dreams come true in
## CASSIE'S COWBOY
by Diane Pershing (on sale April 2002)

A legacy of love arrives
## BECAUSE OF THE RING
by Stella Bagwell (on sale May 2002)

*Available at
your favorite retail outlet.*

*Where love comes alive*™

Visit Silhouette at www.eHarlequin.com
SRSOUL

# buy books

**Your one-stop shop for great reads at great prices. We have all your favorite Harlequin, Silhouette, MIRA and Steeple Hill books, as well as a host of other bestsellers in Other Romances. Discover a wide array of new releases, bargains and hard-to-find books today!**

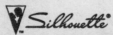

# learn to write

**Become the writer you always knew you could be: get tips and tools on how to craft the perfect romance novel and have your work critiqued by professional experts in romance fiction. Follow your dream now!**

*Silhouette®*

**Where love comes alive™—online...**

Visit us at
**www.eHarlequin.com**

SINTLTW

King Philippe has died, leaving no male heirs to ascend the throne. Until his mother announces that a son *may* exist, embarking everyone on a desperate search for... the missing heir.

Their quest begins March 2002 and continues through June 2002.

On sale March 2002, the emotional
**OF ROYAL BLOOD**
by Carolyn Zane (SR #1576)

On sale April 2002, the intense
**IN PURSUIT OF A PRINCESS**
by Donna Clayton (SR #1582)

On sale May 2002, the heartwarming
**A PRINCESS IN WAITING**
by Carol Grace (SR #1588)

On sale June 2002, the exhilarating
**A PRINCE AT LAST!**
by Cathie Linz (SR #1594)

*Available at your favorite retail outlet.*

*Where love comes alive*™

Visit Silhouette at www.eHarlequin.com
SRRW4